4164

STAR WARS

CLONE WARS

ADVENTURES

VOLUME 1

designer
Darin Fabrick

associate editor
Jeremy Barlow

editor
Randy Stradley

publisher
Mike Richardson

special thanks to Sue Rostoni and Amy Gary
at Lucas Licensing

talk about this book online at: www.darkhorse.com/community/boards

The events in this story take place approximately
five months after the Battle of Geonosis.

Dark Horse Books
A division of Dark Horse Comics, Inc.
10956 S.E. Main Street
Milwaukie, OR 97222

First edition: July 2004
ISBN-10: 1-59307-243-0
ISBN-13: 978-1-59307-243-8

7 9 10 8

STAR WARS

CLONE WARS

ADVENTURES

VOLUME 1

"BLIND FORCE"

script **Haden Blackman**

art and colors **Ben Caldwell**

"HEAVY METAL JEDI"

script **Haden Blackman**

art **The Fillbach Brothers**

colors **Sno Cone Studios, Ltd.**

"FIERCE CURRENTS"

script **Haden Blackman**

art **The Fillbach Brothers**

colors **Sno Cone Studios, Ltd.**

lettering

Michael David Thomas

cover

Ben Caldwell

Dark Horse Books™

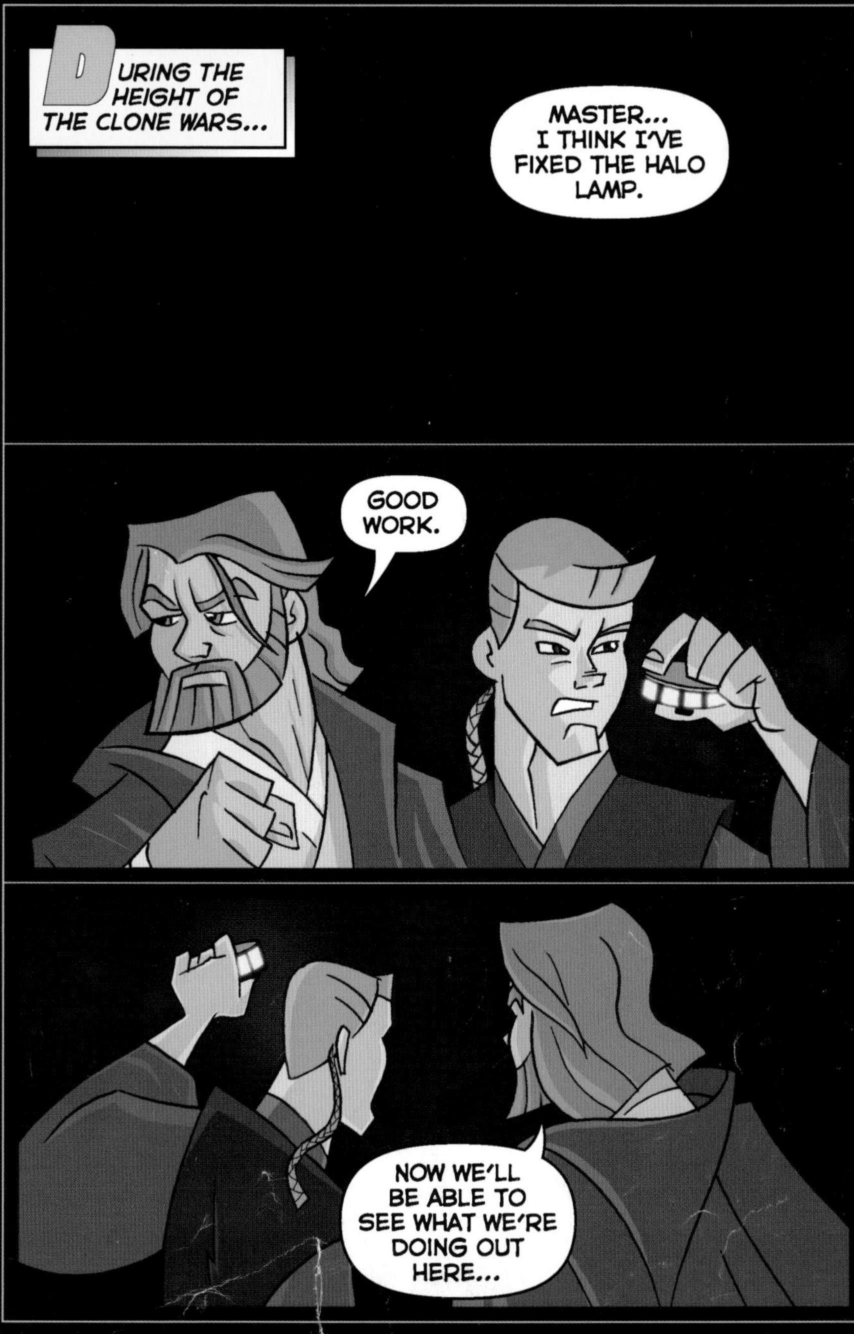
DURING THE HEIGHT OF THE CLONE WARS...
MASTER... I THINK I'VE FIXED THE HALO LAMP.
GOOD WORK.
NOW WE'LL BE ABLE TO SEE WHAT WE'RE DOING OUT HERE...

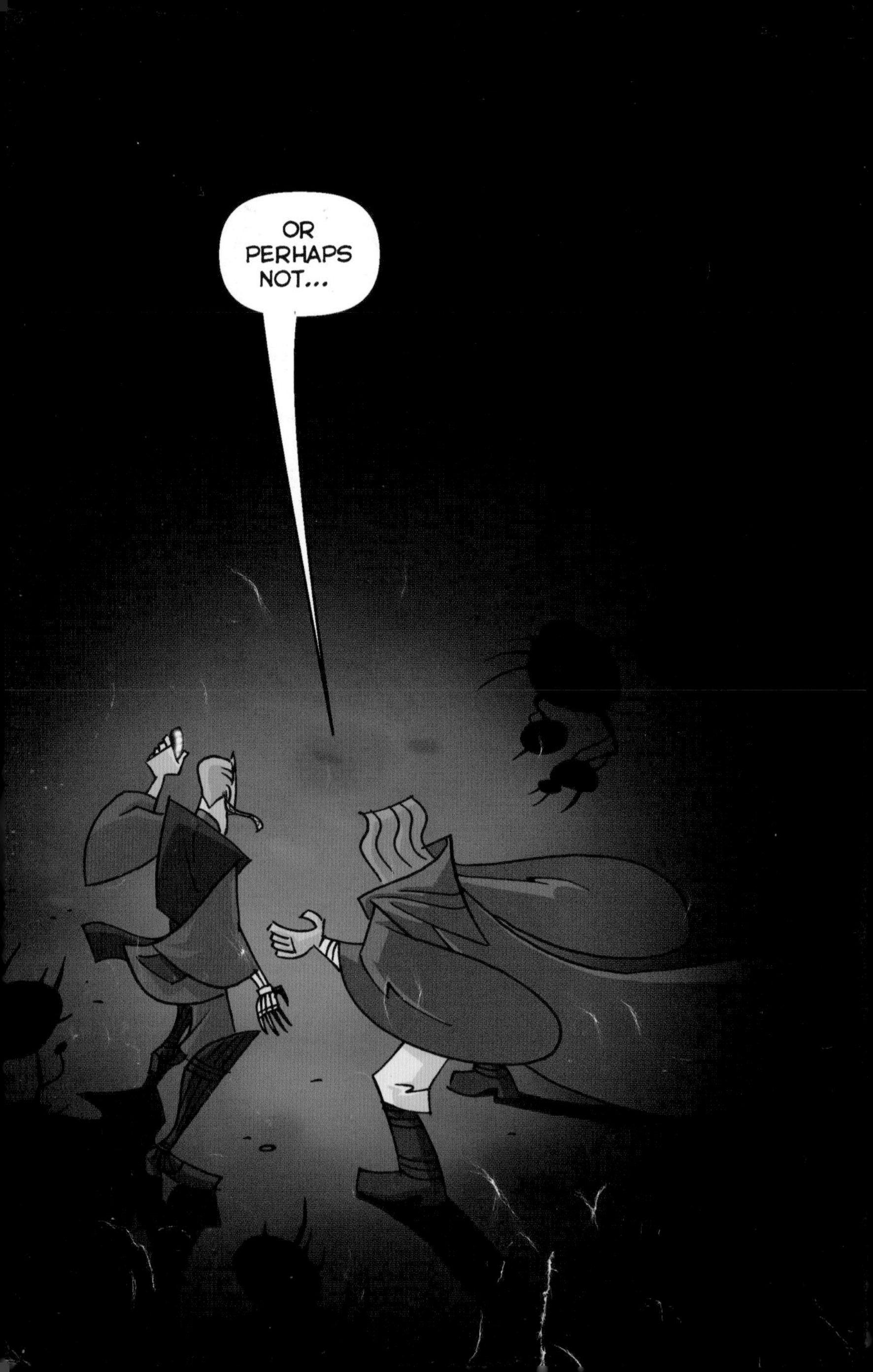
OR PERHAPS NOT...

OBI-WAN KENOBI AND ANAKIN SKYWALKER IN:

BLIND FORCE

A CLONE WARS ADVENTURE

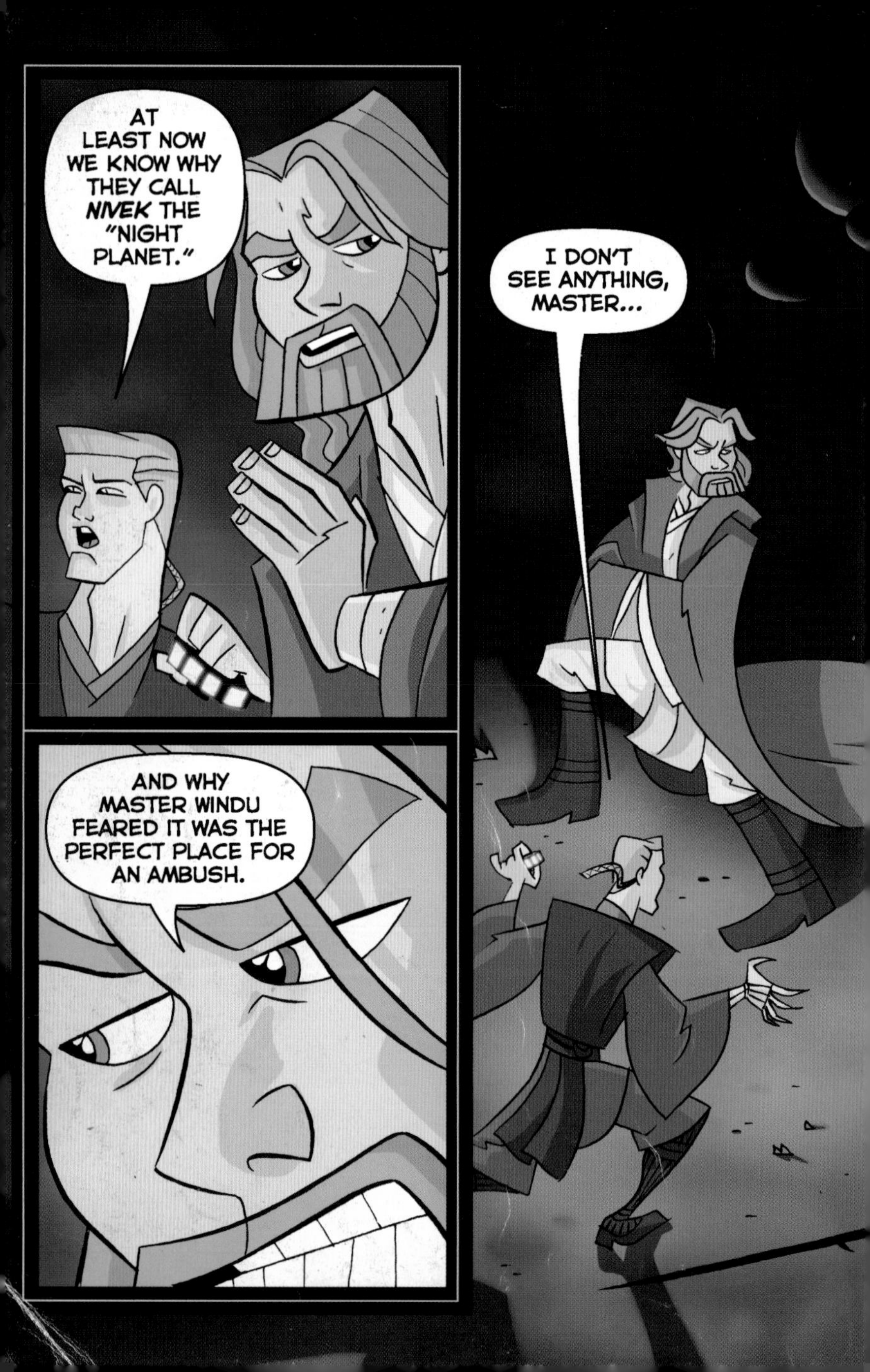
AT LEAST NOW WE KNOW WHY THEY CALL *NIVEK* THE "NIGHT PLANET."
AND WHY MASTER WINDU FEARED IT WAS THE PERFECT PLACE FOR AN AMBUSH.
I DON'T SEE ANYTHING, MASTER...

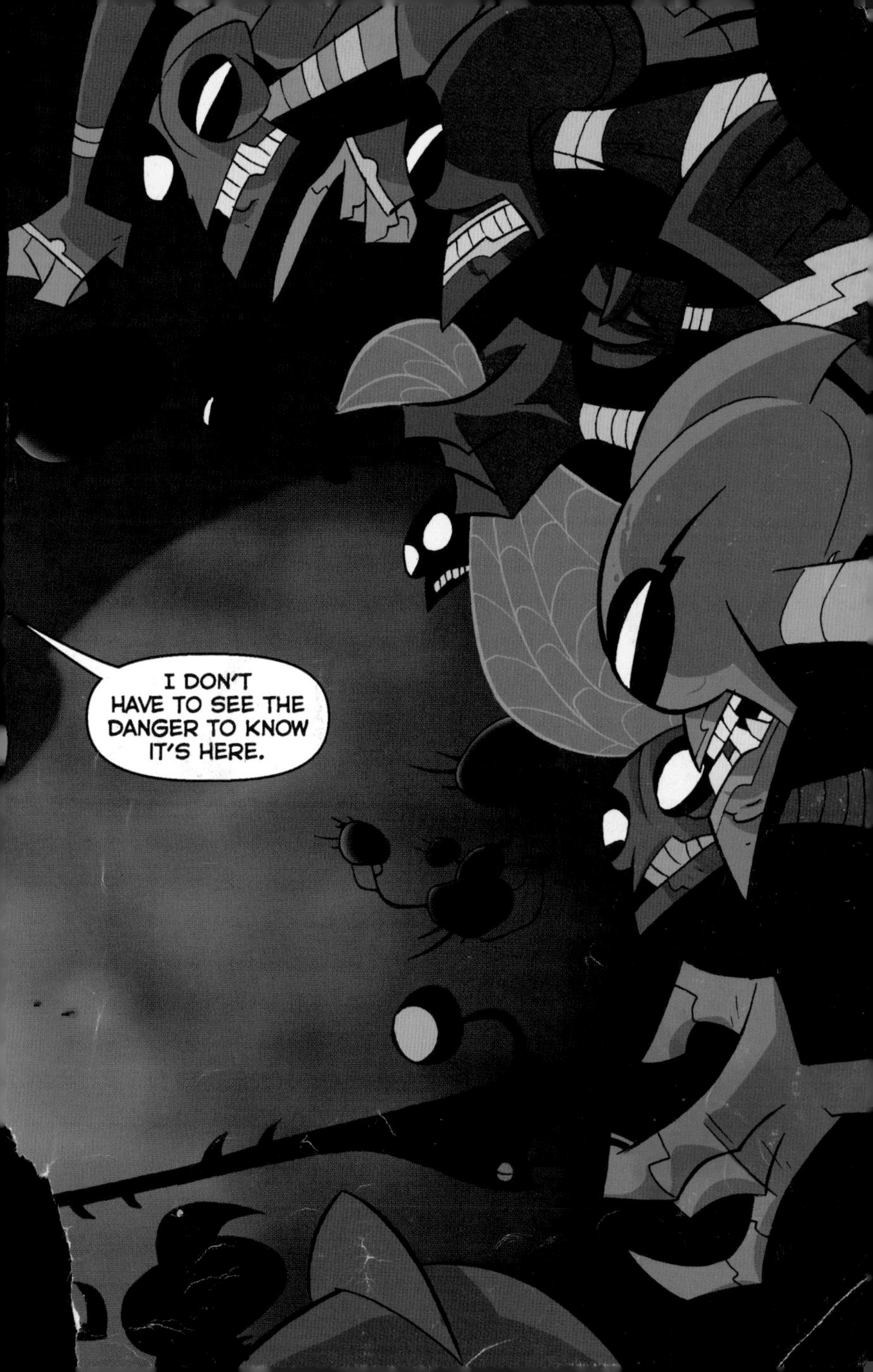
I DON'T HAVE TO SEE THE DANGER TO KNOW IT'S HERE.

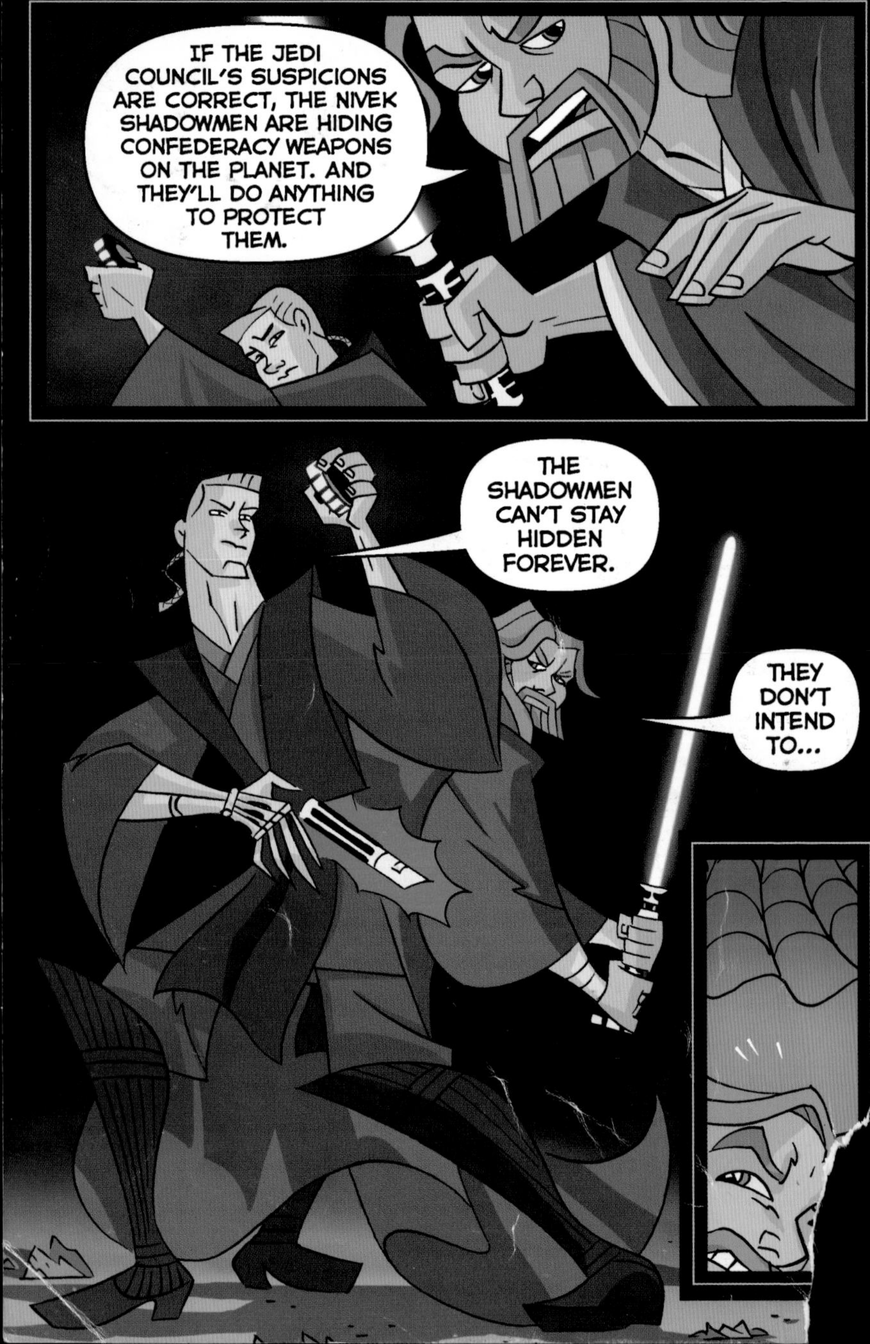
IF THE JEDI COUNCIL'S SUSPICIONS ARE CORRECT, THE NIVEK SHADOWMEN ARE HIDING CONFEDERACY WEAPONS ON THE PLANET. AND THEY'LL DO ANYTHING TO PROTECT THEM.
THE SHADOWMEN CAN'T STAY HIDDEN FOREVER.
THEY DON'T INTEND TO...

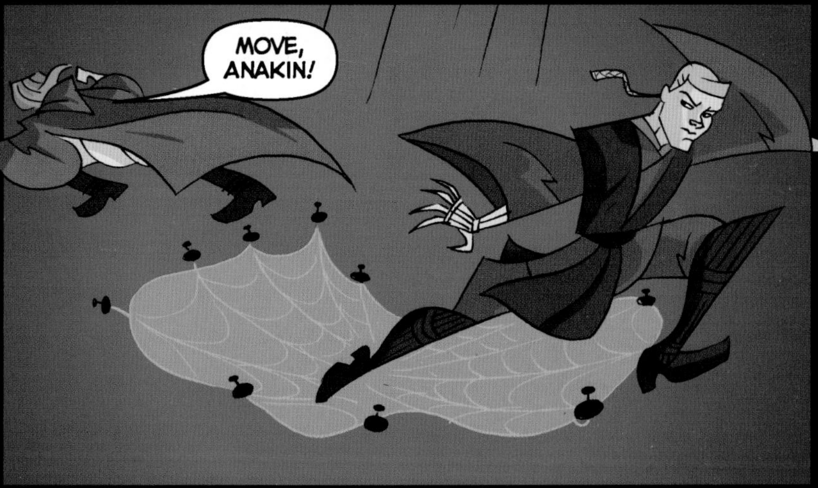
MOVE, ANAKIN!

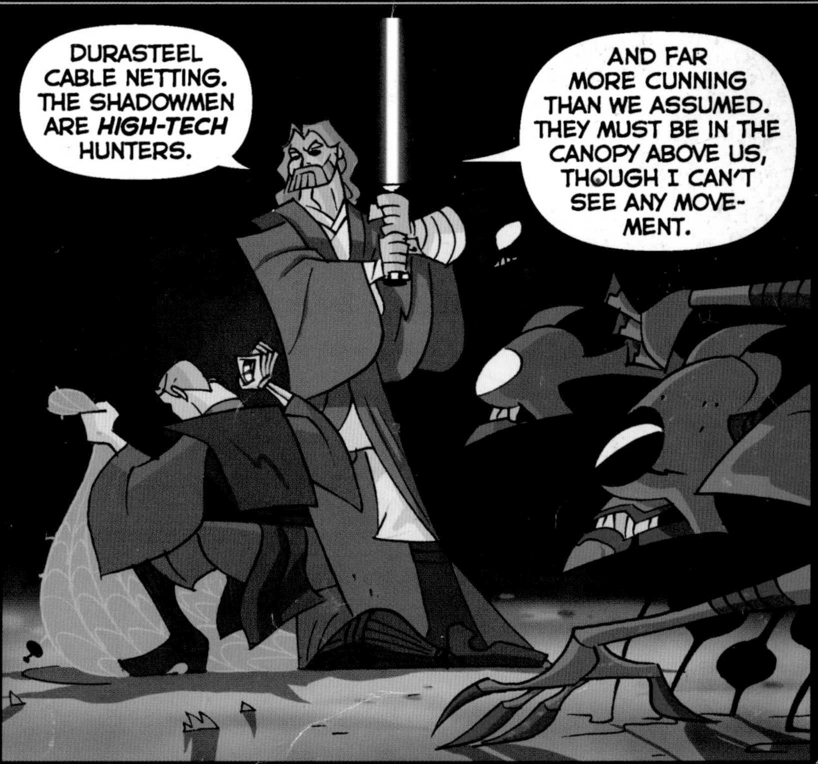
DURASTEEL CABLE NETTING. THE SHADOWMEN ARE *HIGH-TECH* HUNTERS.
AND FAR MORE CUNNING THAN WE ASSUMED. THEY MUST BE IN THE CANOPY ABOVE US, THOUGH I CAN'T SEE ANY MOVE- MENT.

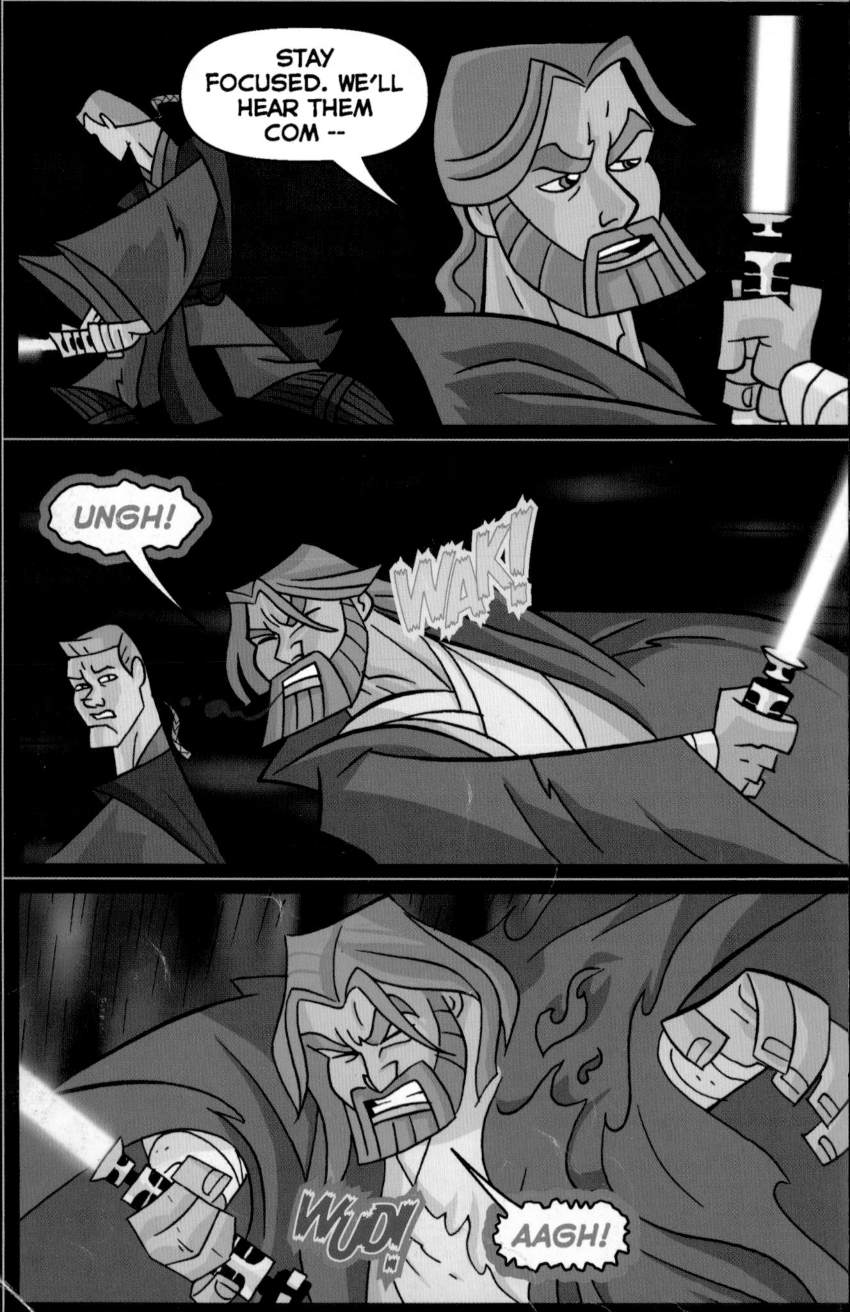
STAY FOCUSED. WE'LL HEAR THEM COM --
UNGH!
WAK!
WUD!
AAGH!

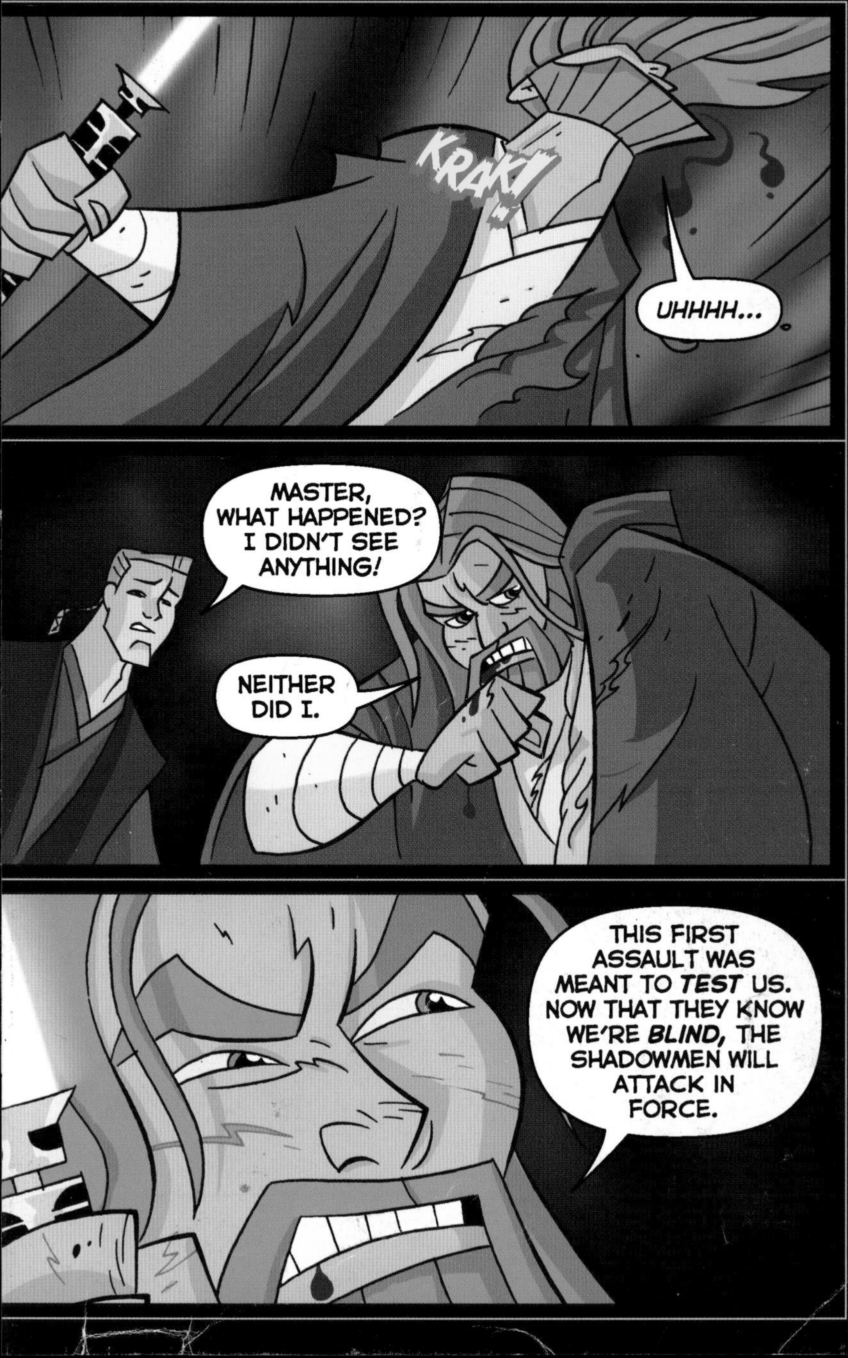
KRAK!
UHHHH...
MASTER, WHAT HAPPENED? I DIDN'T SEE ANYTHING!
NEITHER DID I.
THIS FIRST ASSAULT WAS MEANT TO TEST US. NOW THAT THEY KNOW WE'RE BLIND, THE SHADOWMEN WILL ATTACK IN FORCE.

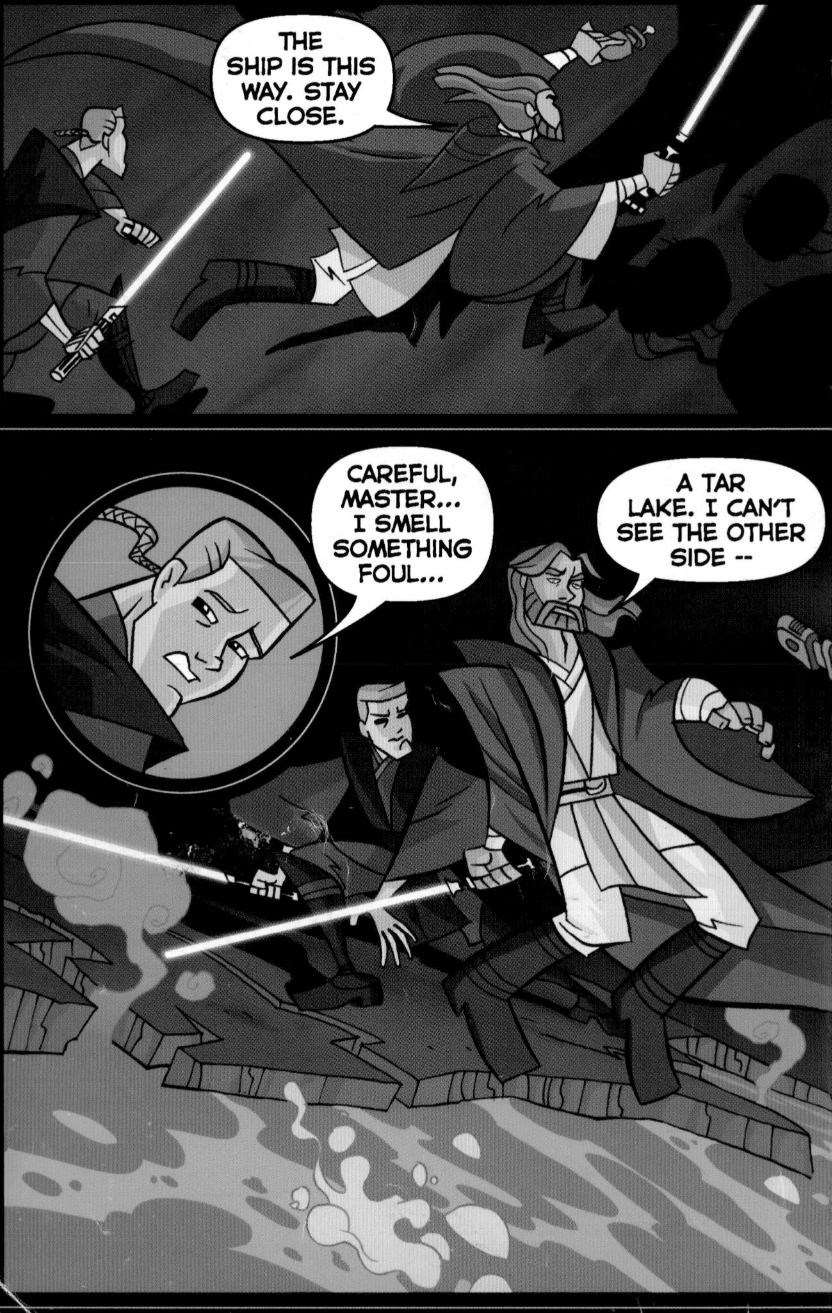
THE SHIP IS THIS WAY. STAY CLOSE.
CAREFUL, MASTER... I SMELL SOMETHING FOUL...
A TAR LAKE. I CAN'T SEE THE OTHER SIDE --

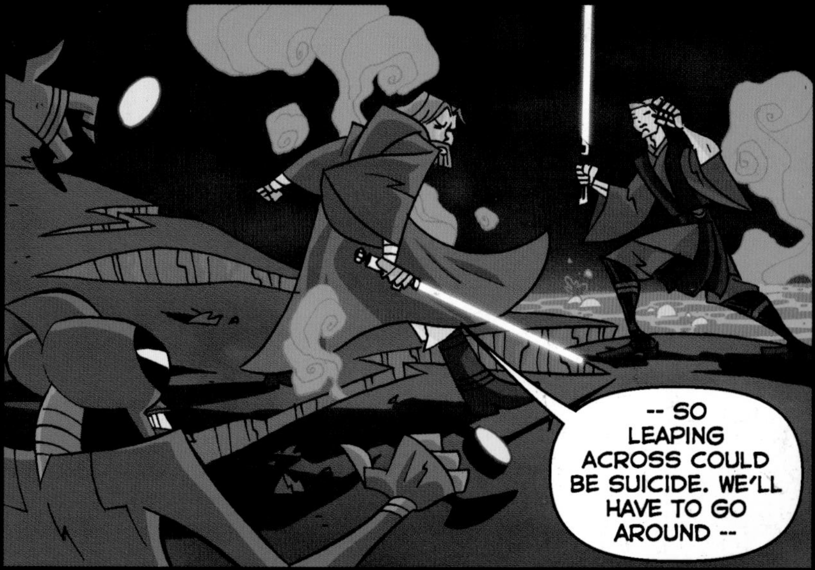
-- SO LEAPING ACROSS COULD BE SUICIDE. WE'LL HAVE TO GO AROUND --

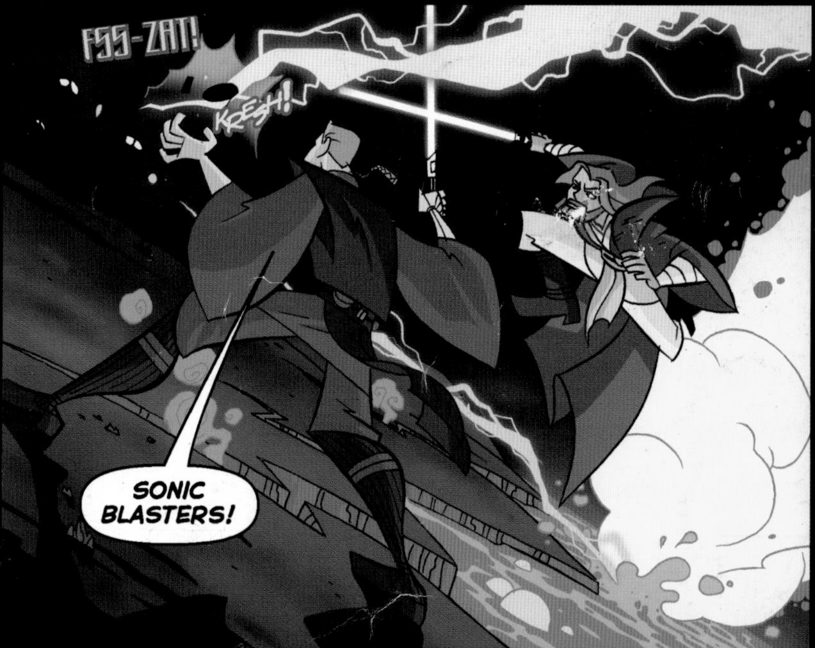
FSS-ZAT!
KRESH!
SONIC BLASTERS!

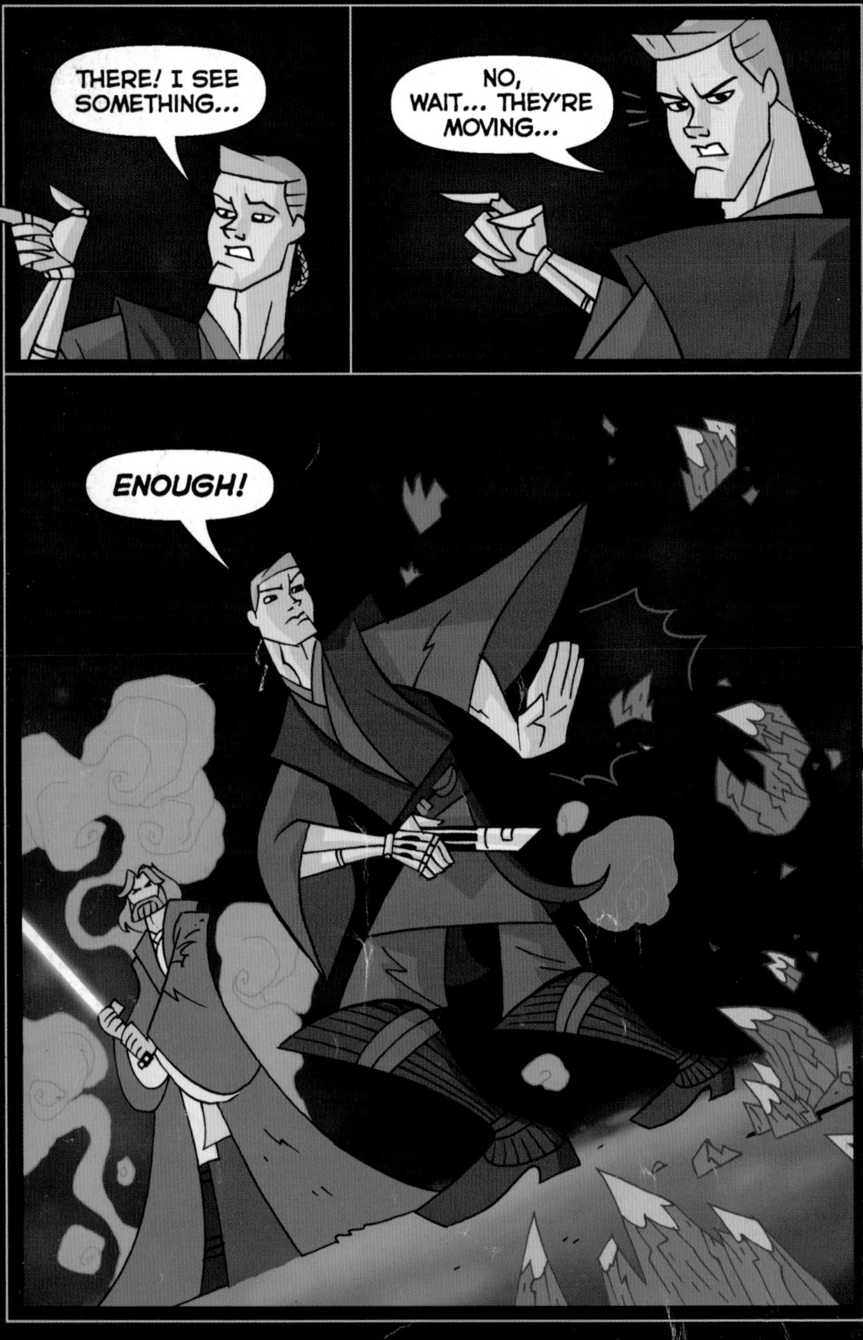
THERE! I SEE SOMETHING...
NO, WAIT... THEY'RE MOVING...
ENOUGH!

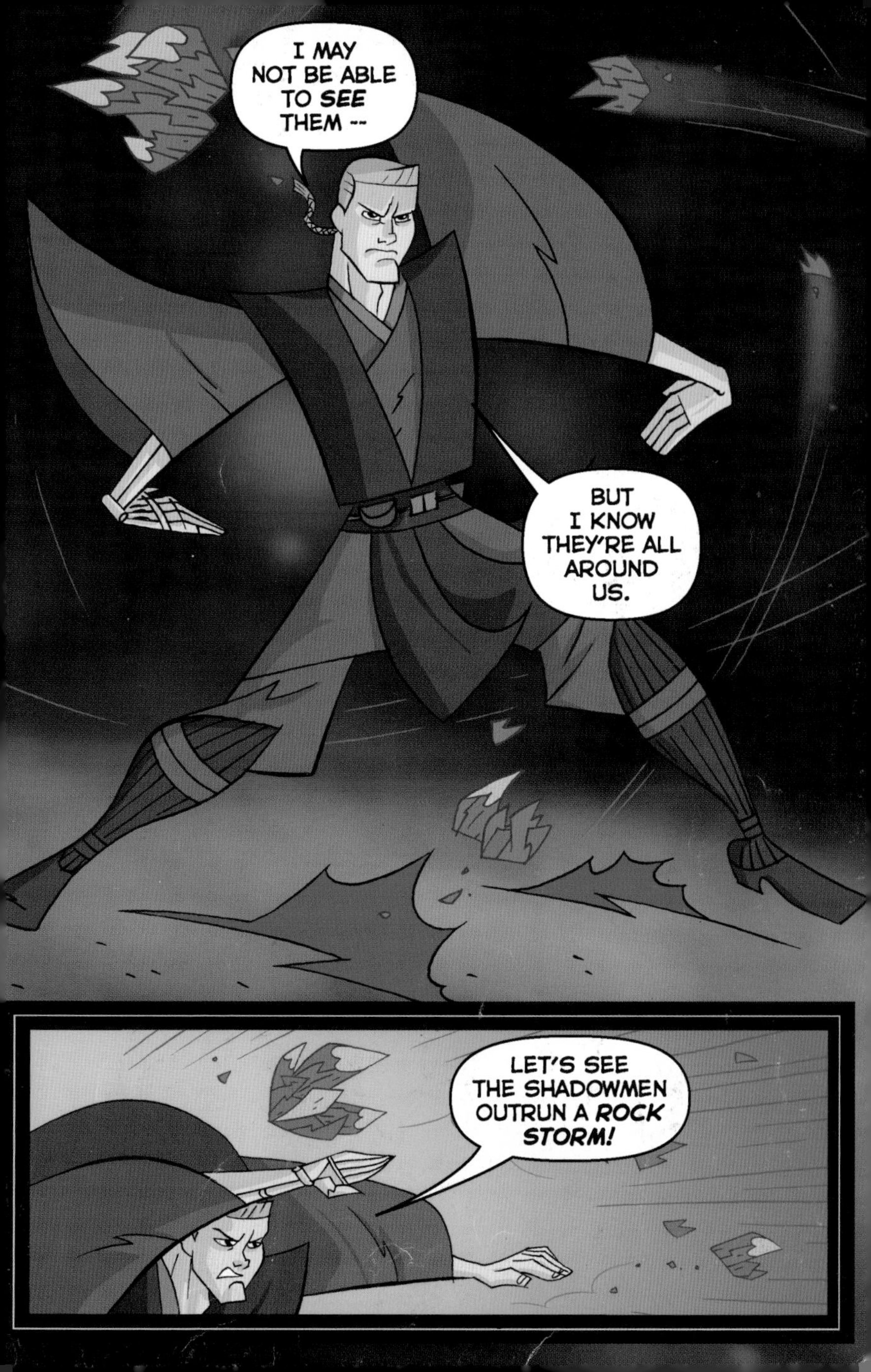
I MAY NOT BE ABLE TO SEE THEM --
BUT I KNOW THEY'RE ALL AROUND US.
LET'S SEE THE SHADOWMEN OUTRUN A ROCK STORM!

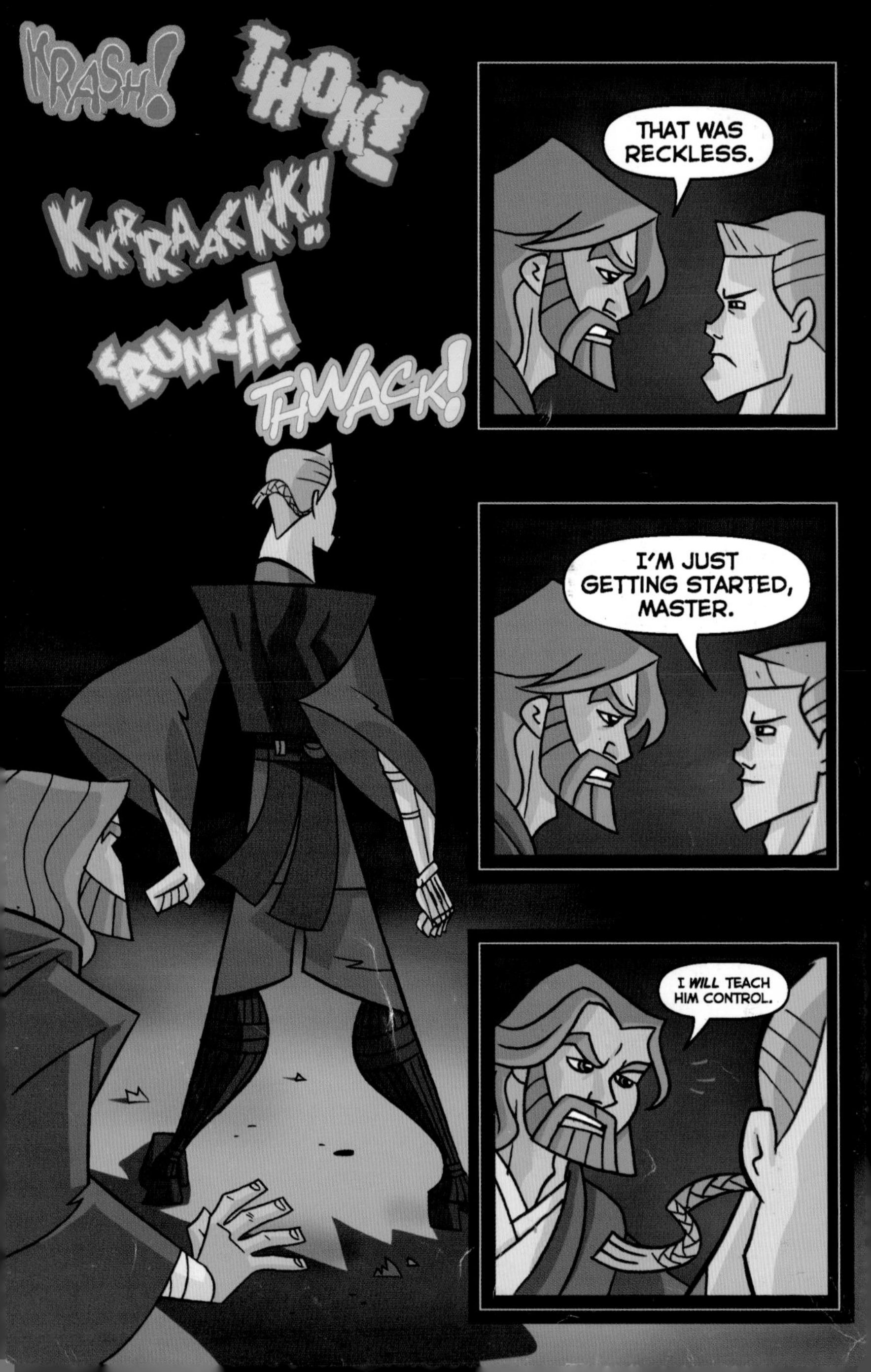
KRASH!
THOK!
KKRRAKK!!
CRUNCH!
THWACK!
THAT WAS RECKLESS.
I'M JUST GETTING STARTED, MASTER.
I WILL TEACH HIM CONTROL.

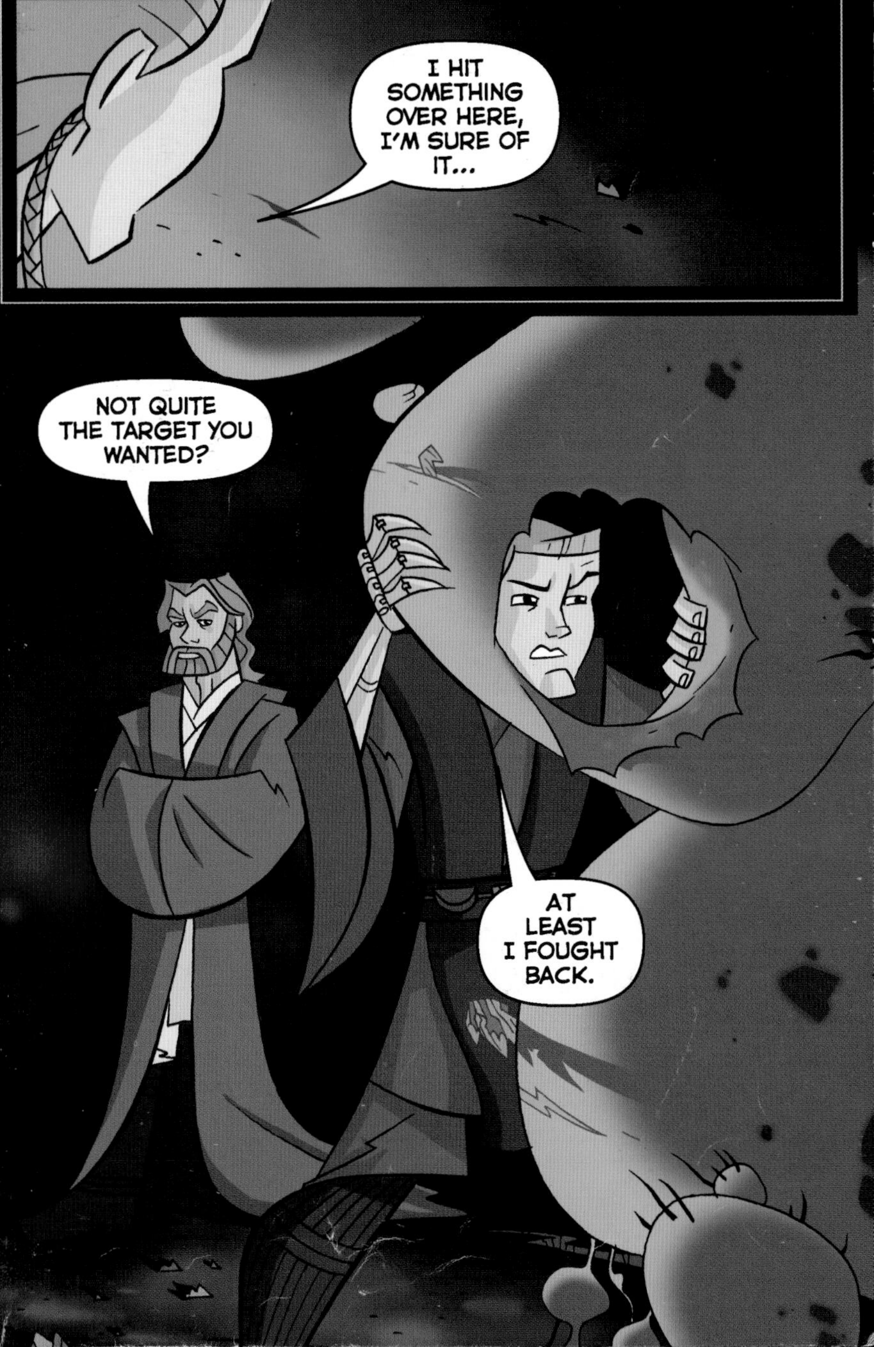
I HIT SOMETHING OVER HERE, I'M SURE OF IT...
NOT QUITE THE TARGET YOU WANTED?
AT LEAST I FOUGHT BACK.

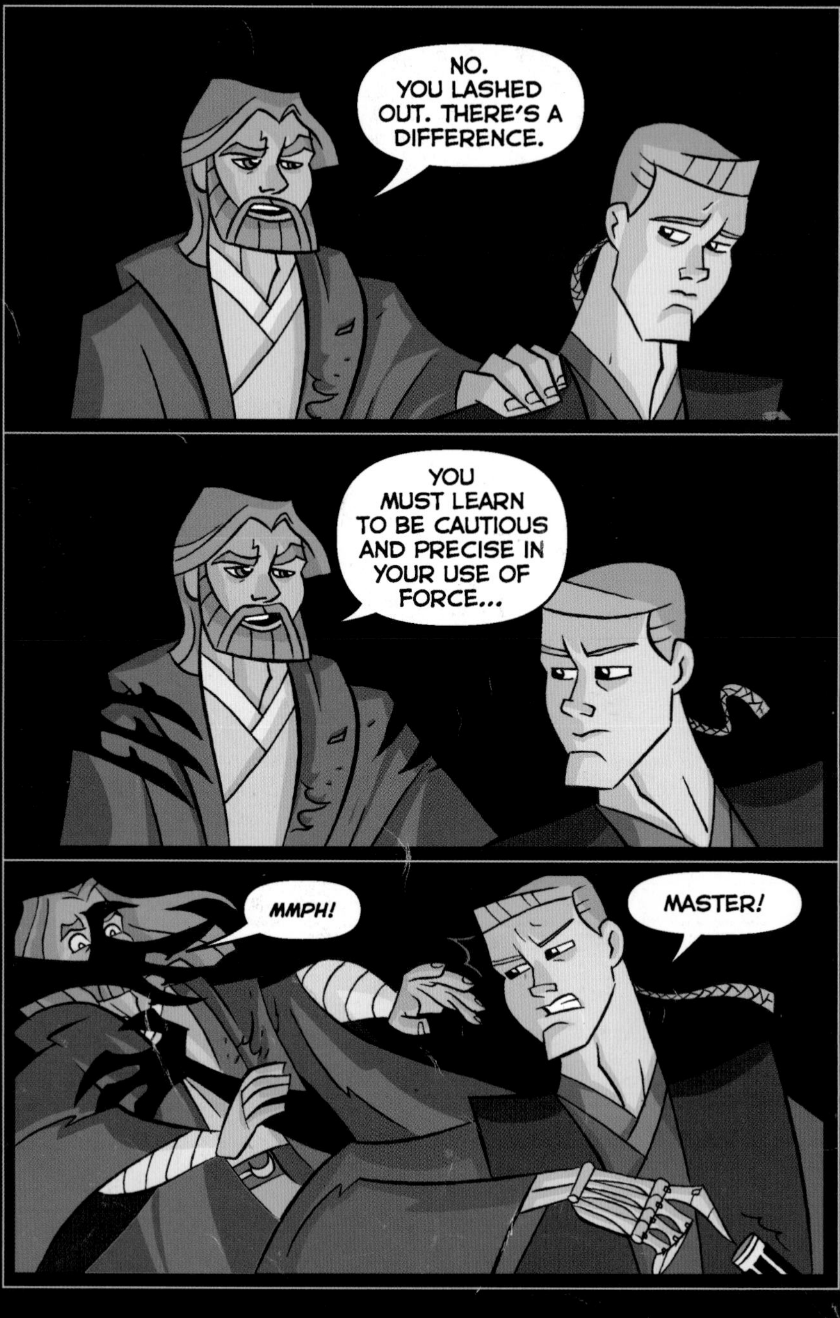
NO.
YOU LASHED OUT. THERE'S A DIFFERENCE.
YOU MUST LEARN TO BE CAUTIOUS AND PRECISE IN YOUR USE OF FORCE...
MMPH!
MASTER!

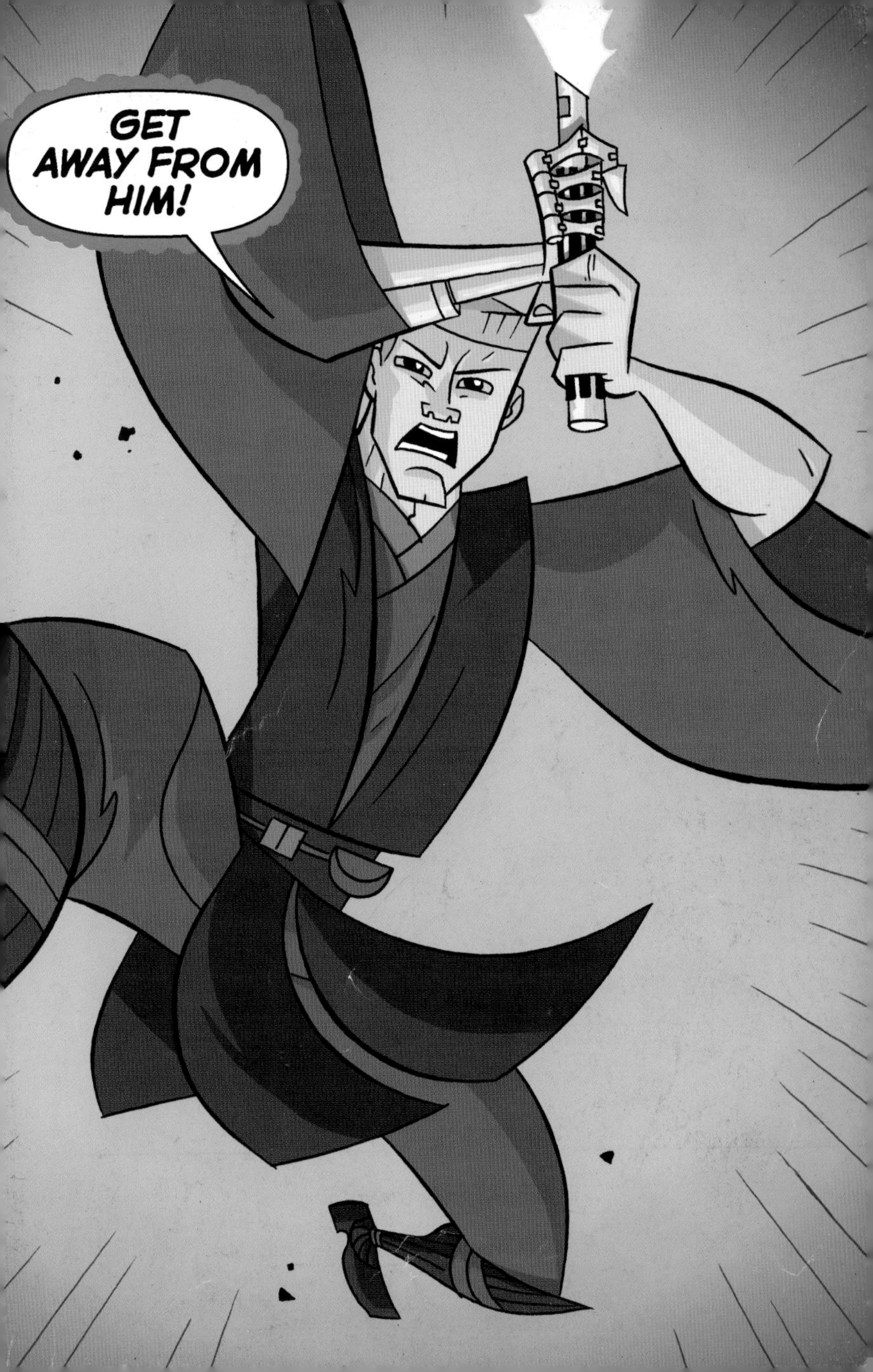
GET AWAY FROM HIM!

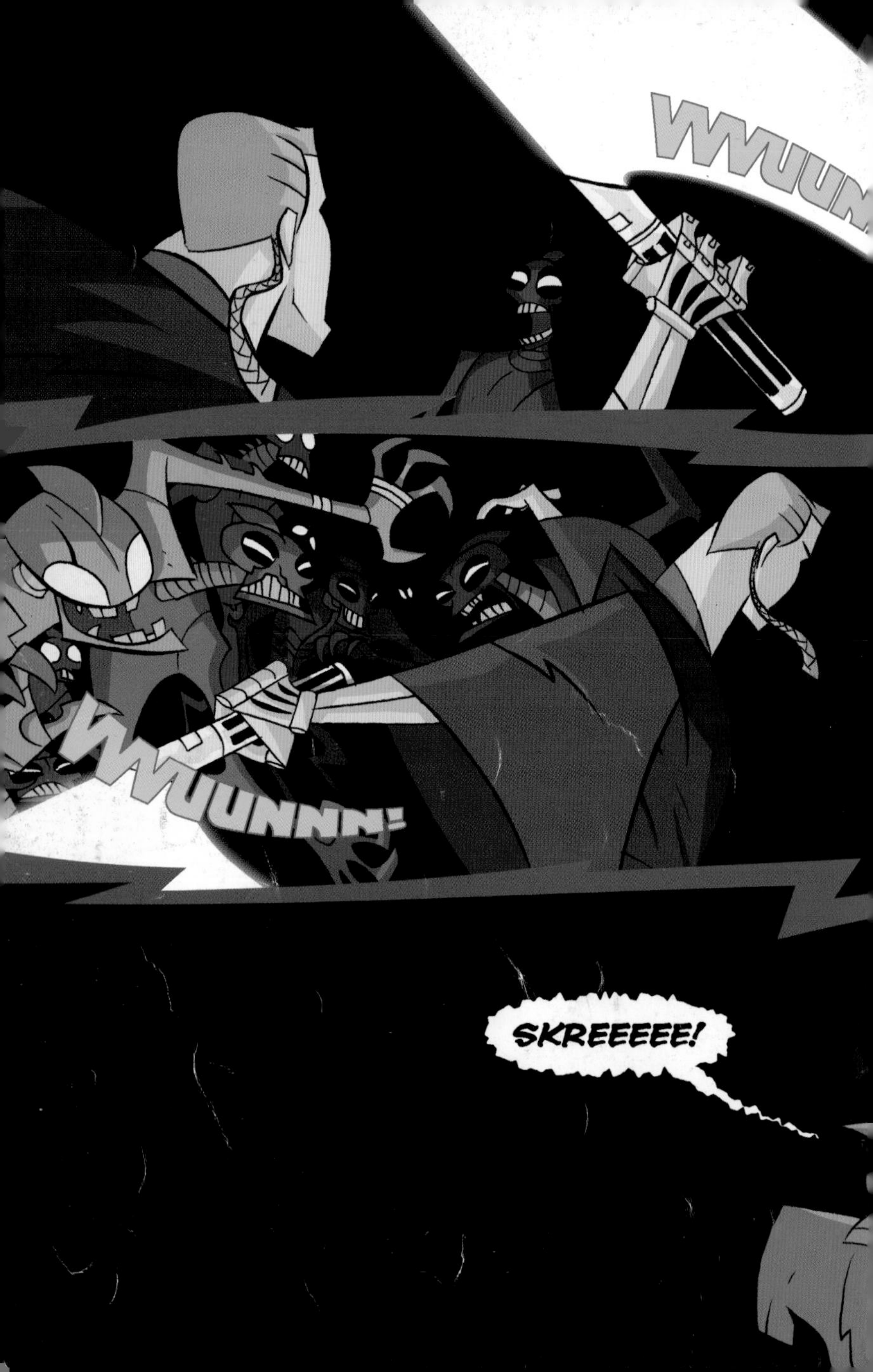
WWUUN
WWUUNNN!
SKREEEEEE!

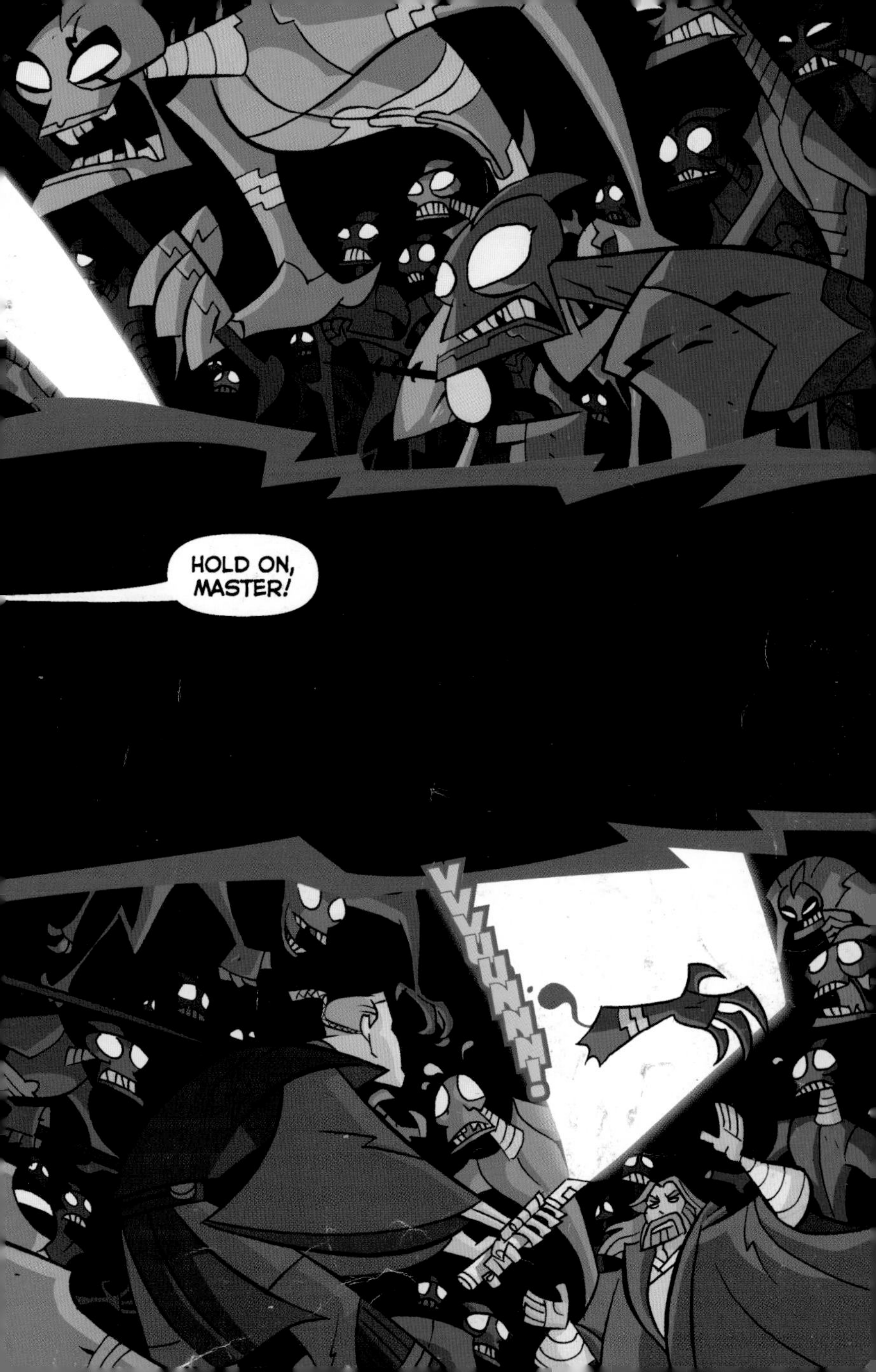
HOLD ON, MASTER!
VVVUUNNN!

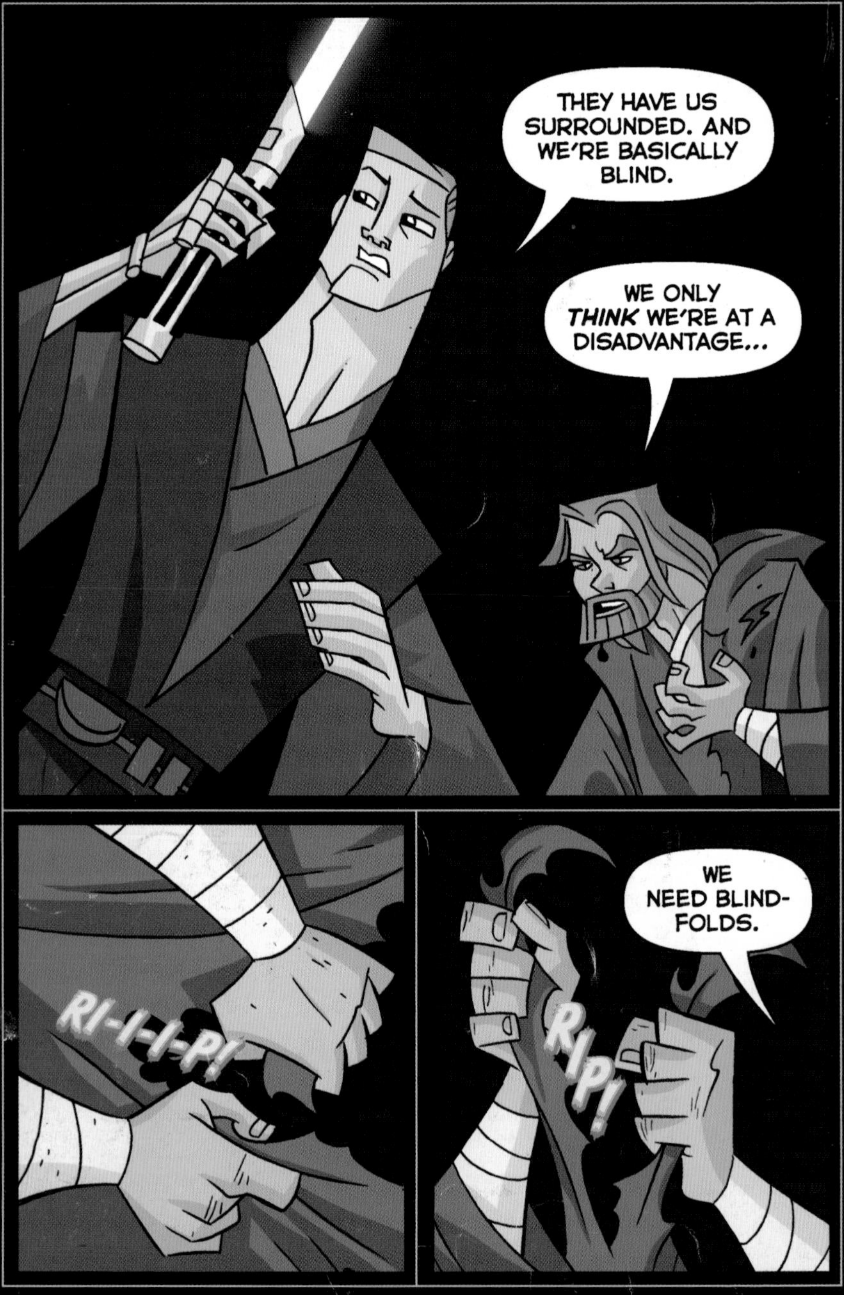
THEY HAVE US SURROUNDED. AND WE'RE BASICALLY BLIND.
WE ONLY *THINK* WE'RE AT A DISADVANTAGE...
RI-I-I-P!
WE NEED BLIND-FOLDS.
RIP!

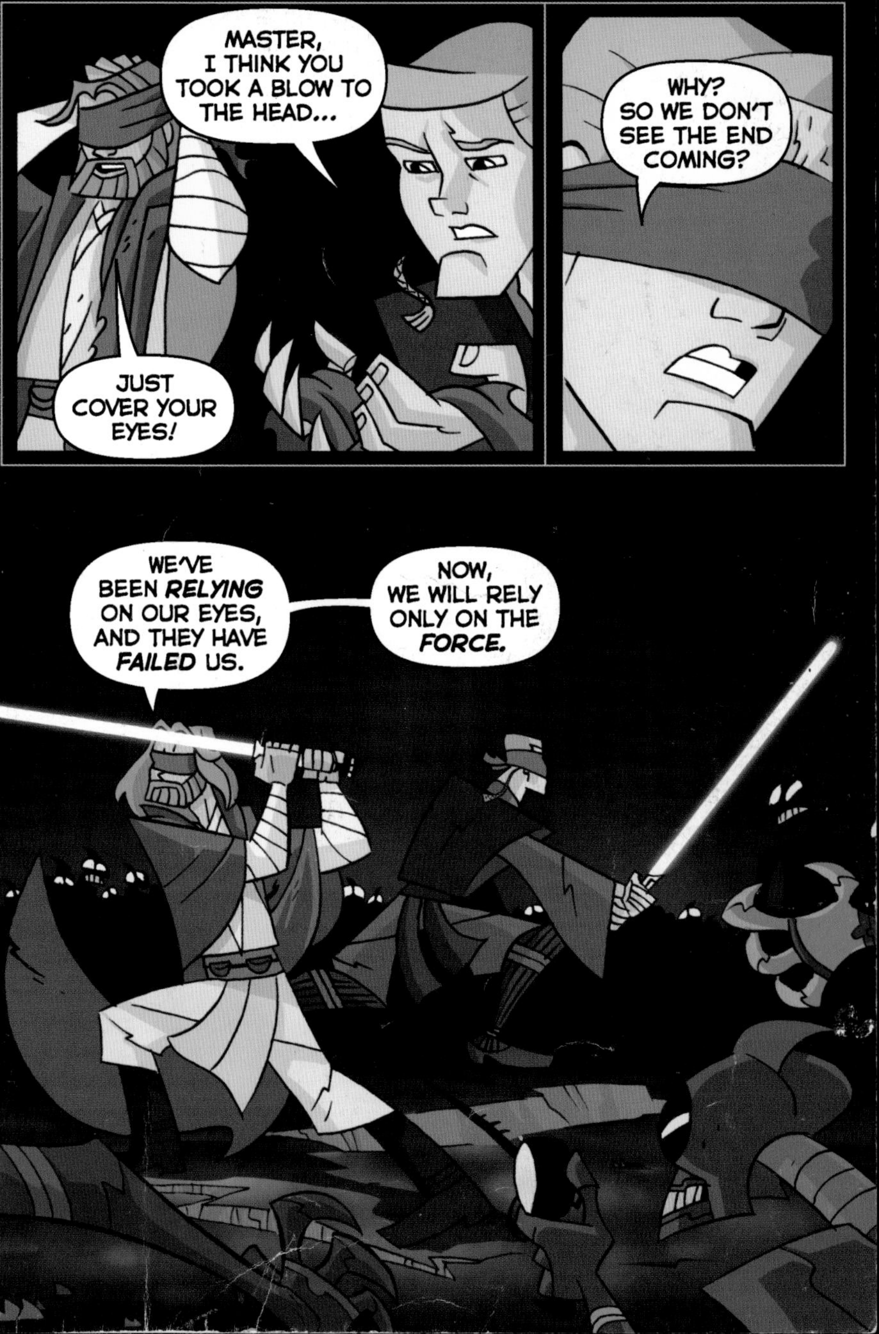
MASTER, I THINK YOU TOOK A BLOW TO THE HEAD...
JUST COVER YOUR EYES!
WHY? SO WE DON'T SEE THE END COMING?
WE'VE BEEN *RELYING* ON OUR EYES, AND THEY HAVE *FAILED* US.
NOW, WE WILL RELY ONLY ON THE *FORCE.*

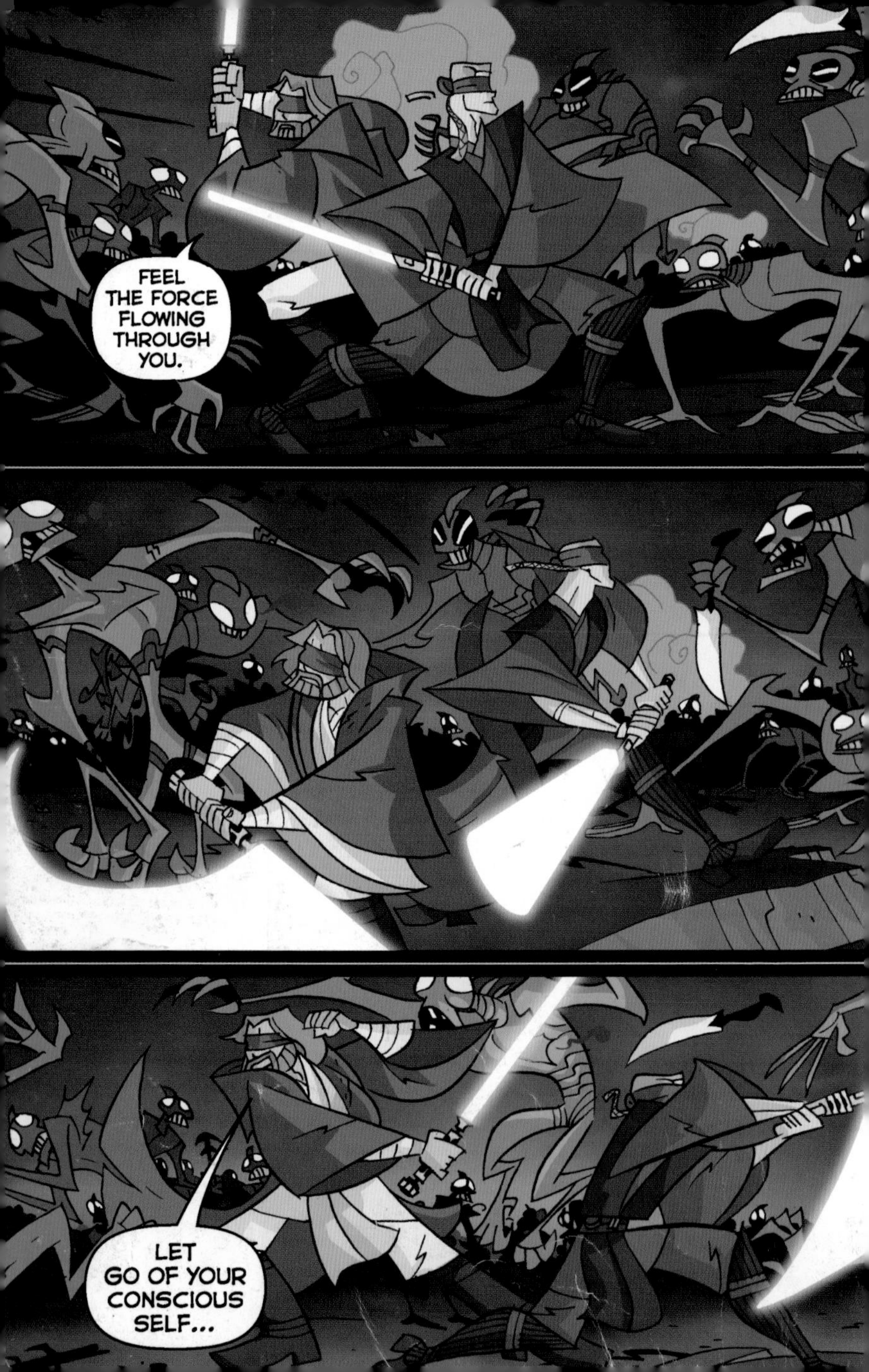
FEEL THE FORCE FLOWING THROUGH YOU.
LET GO OF YOUR CONSCIOUS SELF...

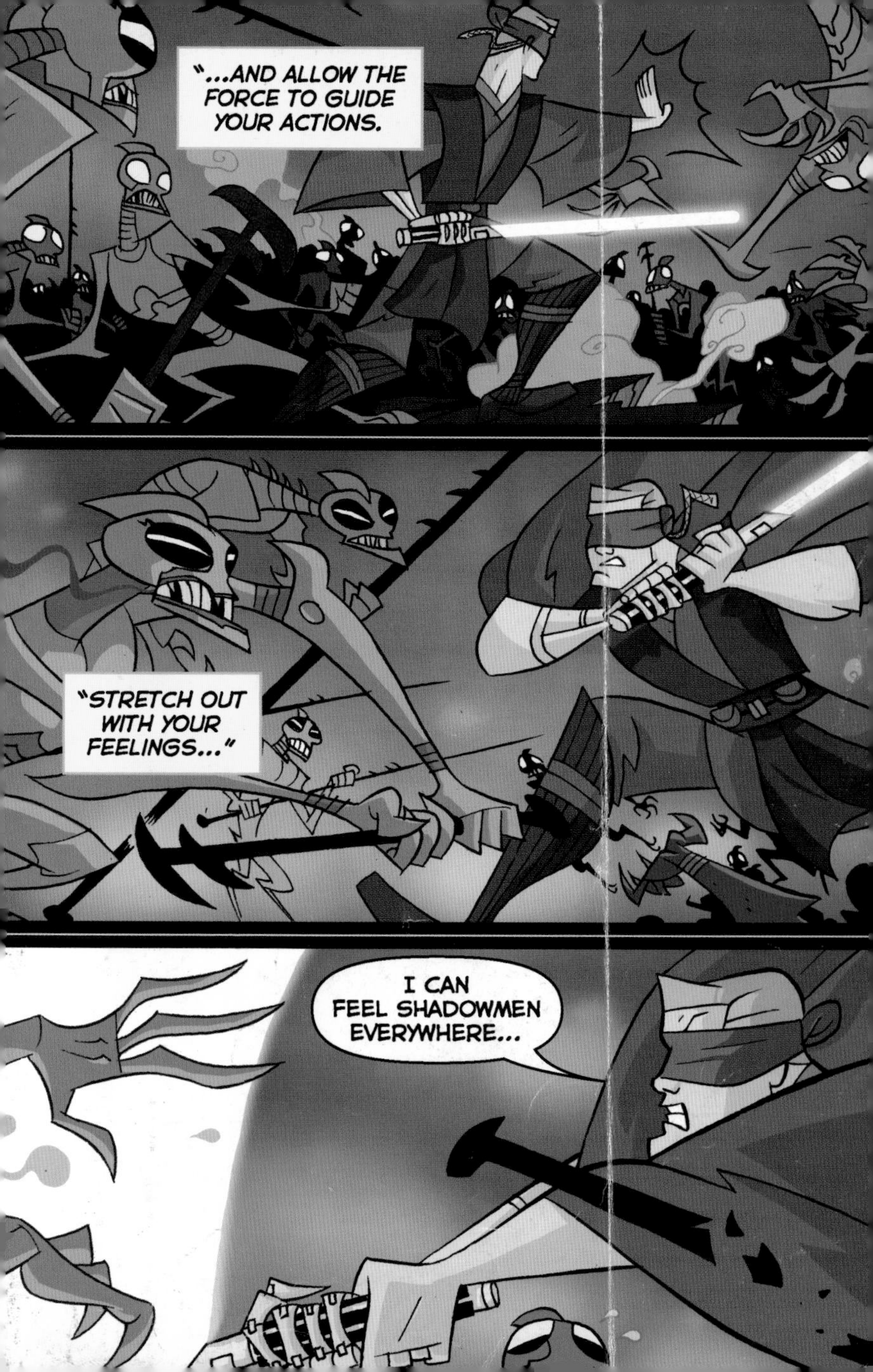
"...AND ALLOW THE FORCE TO GUIDE YOUR ACTIONS.
"STRETCH OUT WITH YOUR FEELINGS..."
I CAN FEEL SHADOWMEN EVERYWHERE...

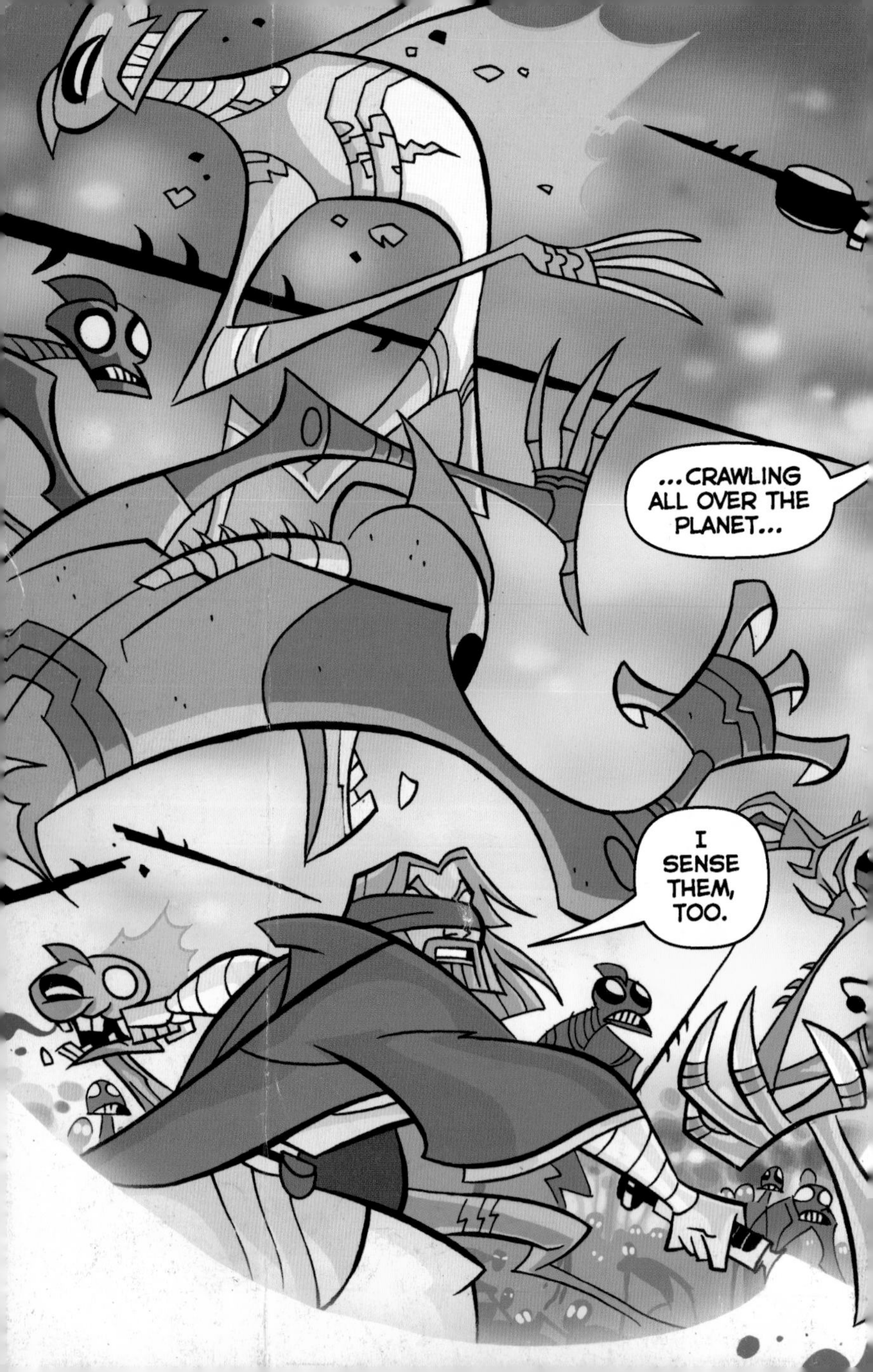
...CRAWLING ALL OVER THE PLANET...
I SENSE THEM, TOO.

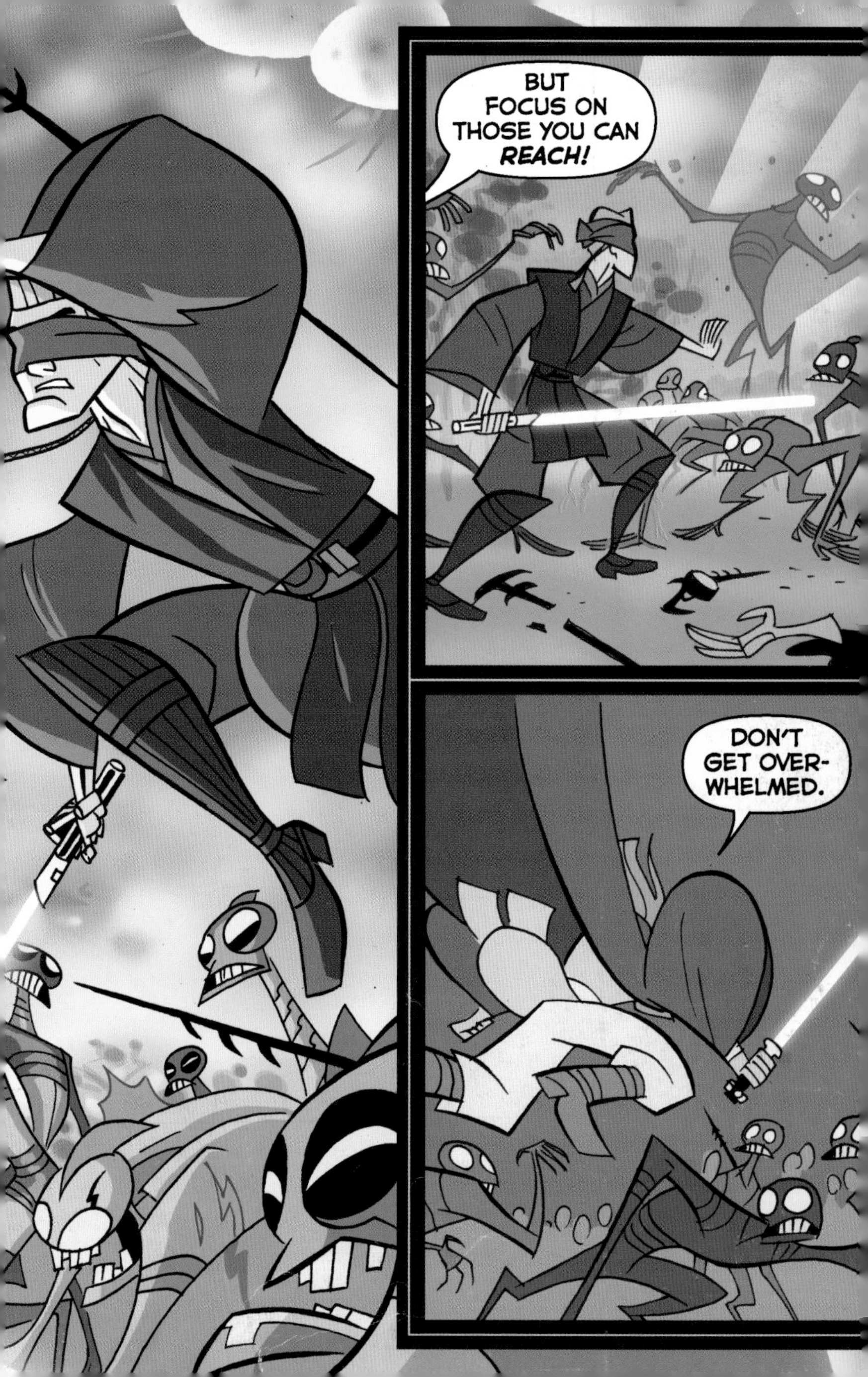
BUT FOCUS ON THOSE YOU CAN *REACH!*
DON'T GET OVER-WHELMED.

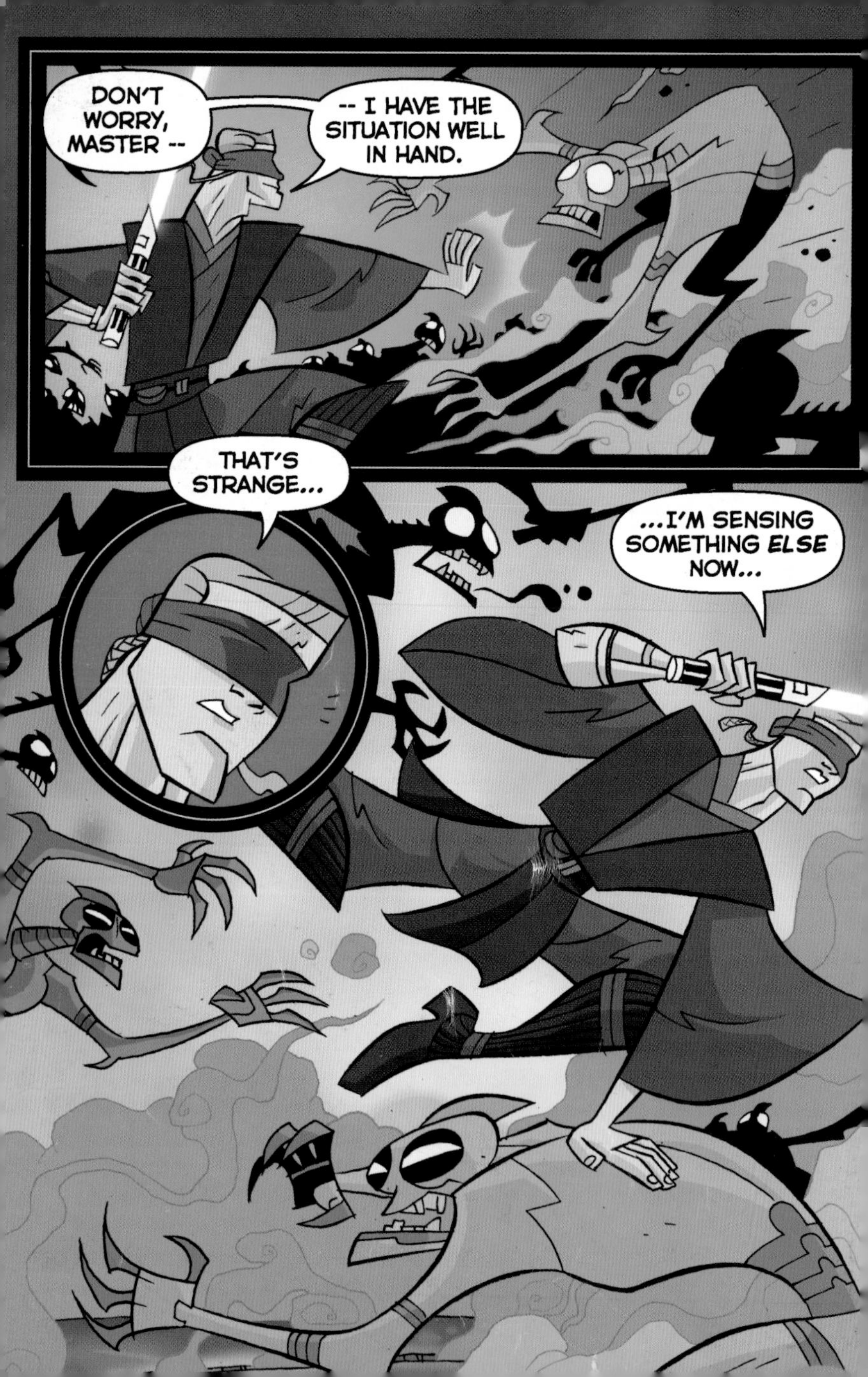
DON'T WORRY, MASTER --
-- I HAVE THE SITUATION WELL IN HAND.
THAT'S STRANGE...
...I'M SENSING SOMETHING ELSE NOW...

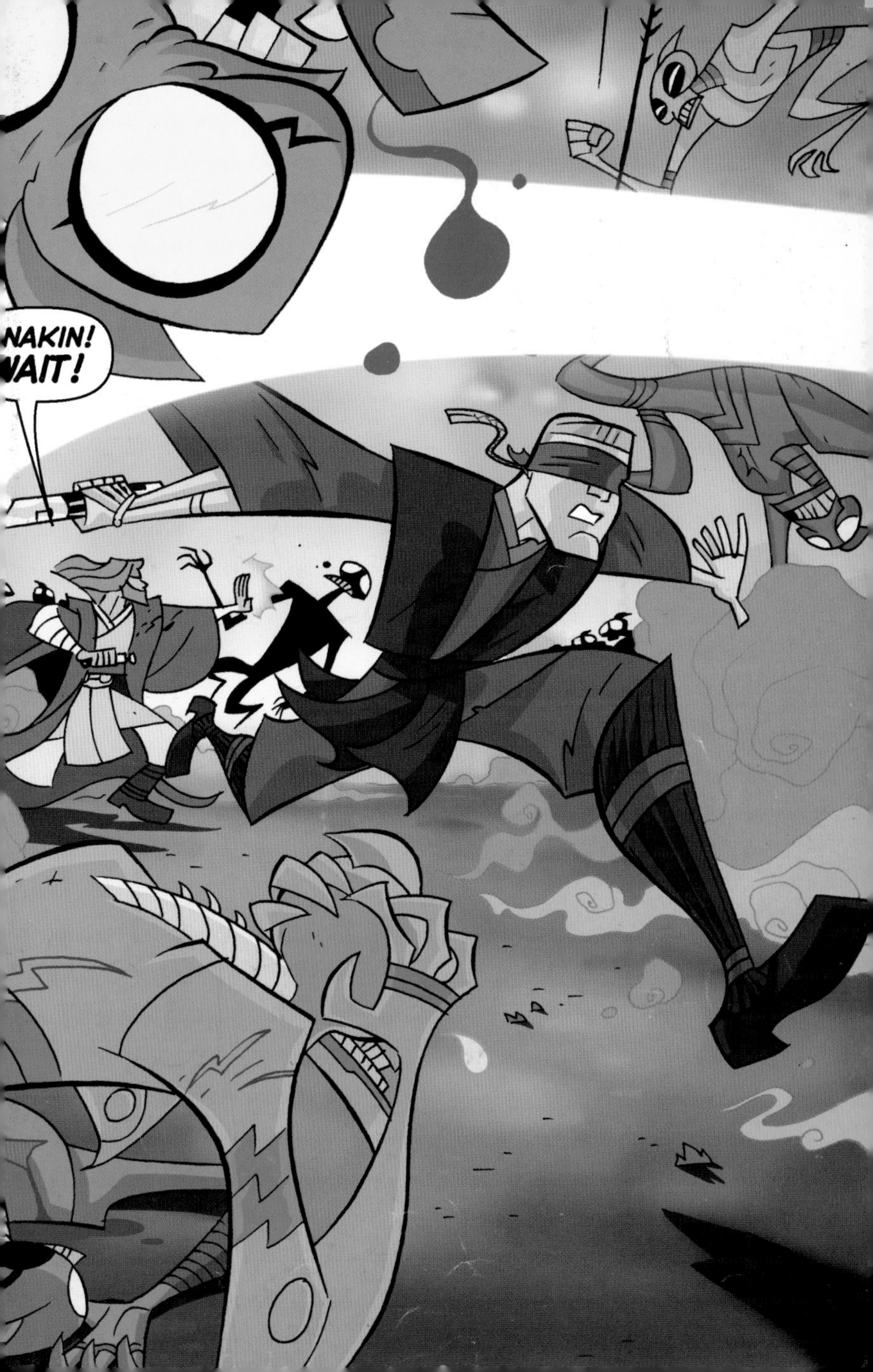
NAKIN!
AIT!

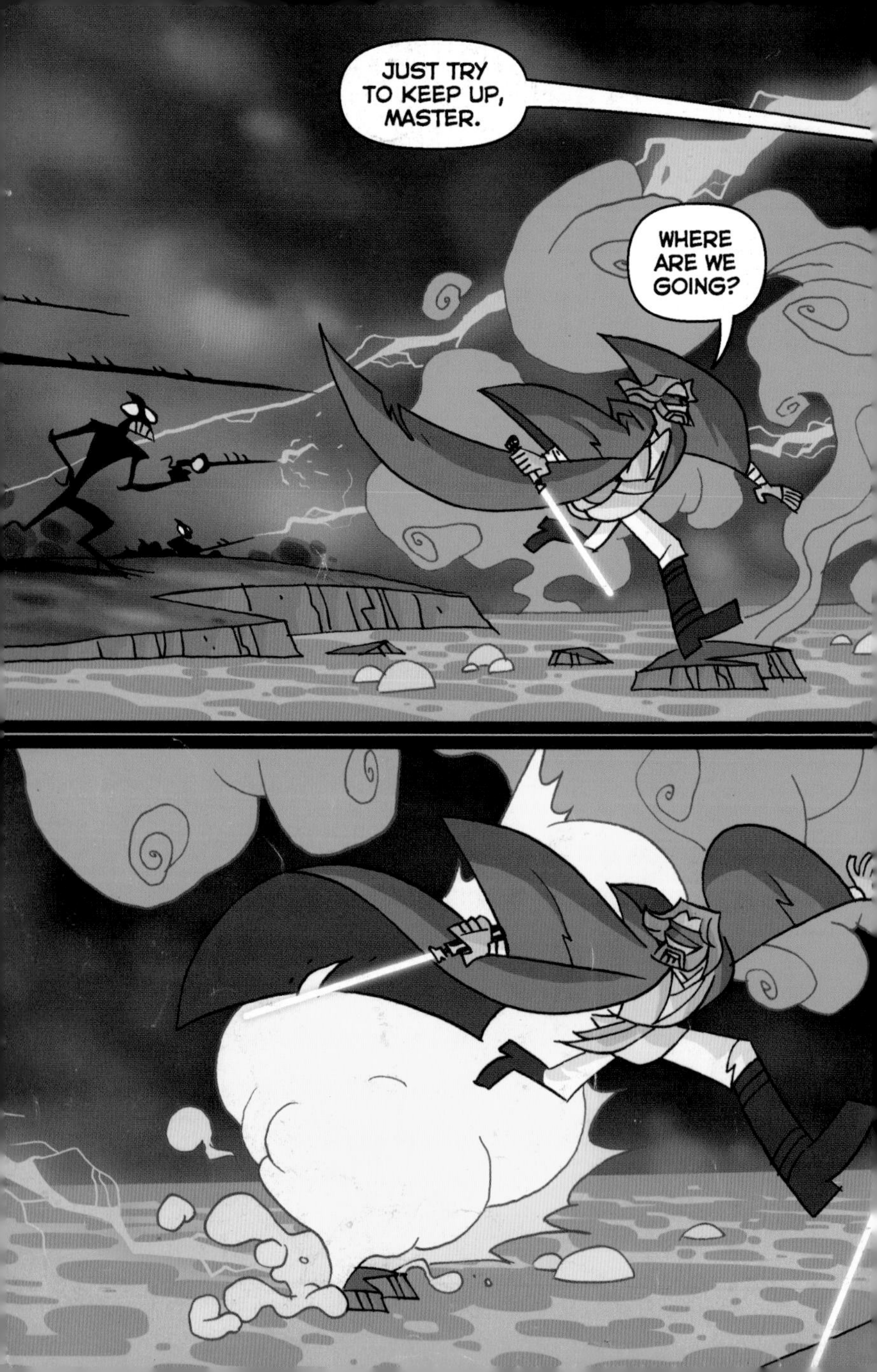
JUST TRY TO KEEP UP, MASTER.
WHERE ARE WE GOING?

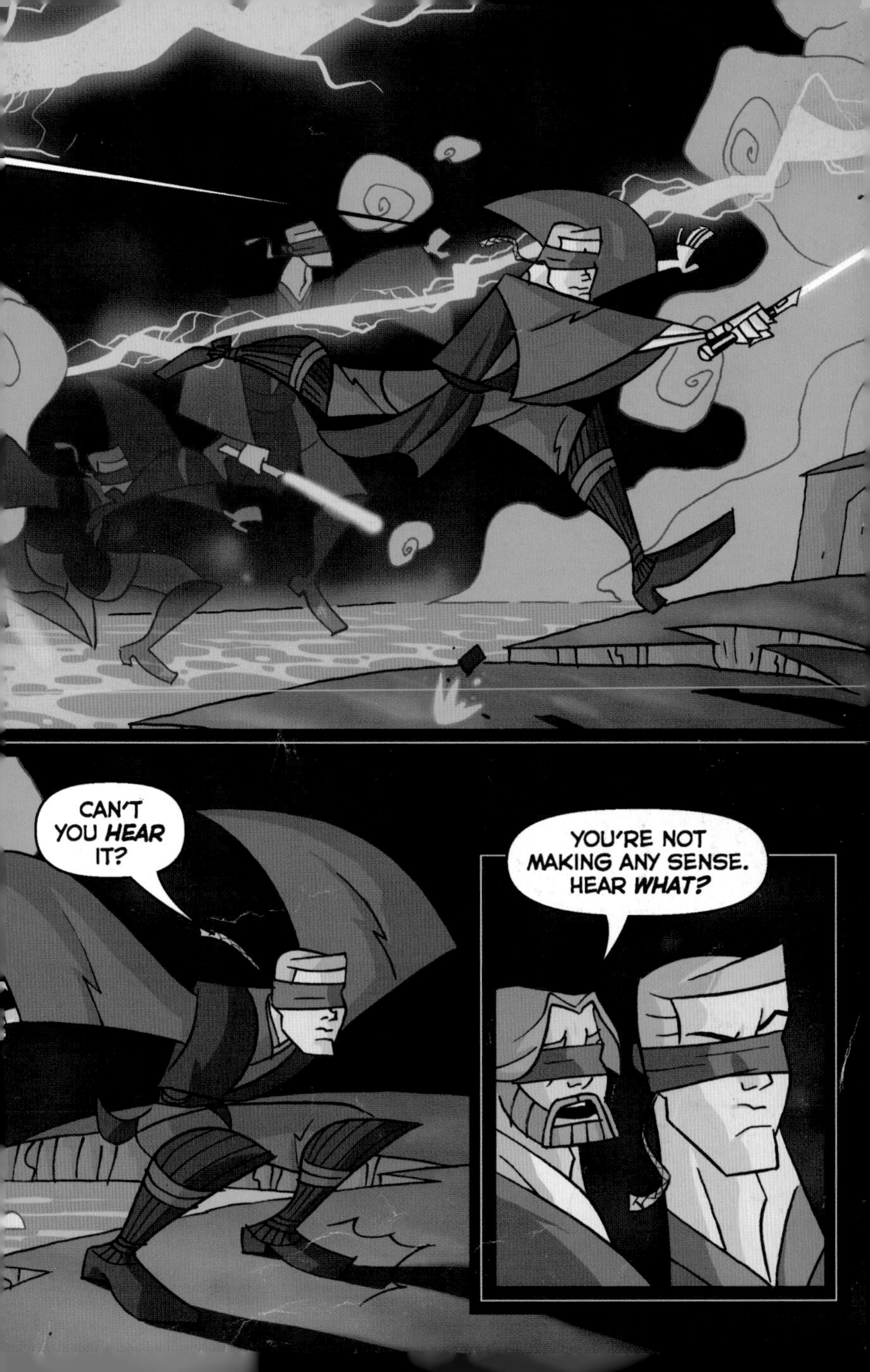
CAN'T YOU *HEAR* IT?
YOU'RE NOT MAKING ANY SENSE. HEAR *WHAT?*

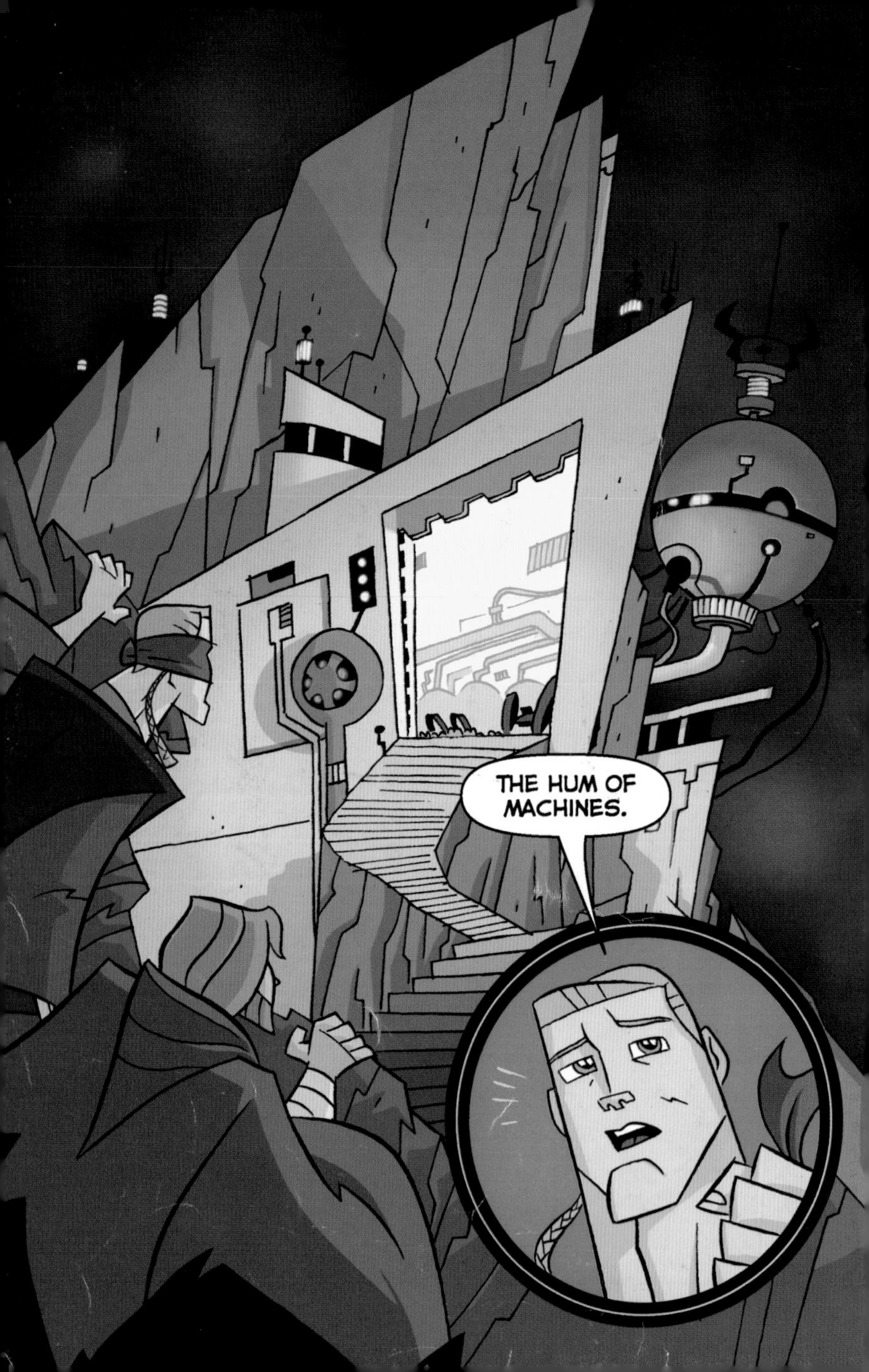
THE HUM OF MACHINES.

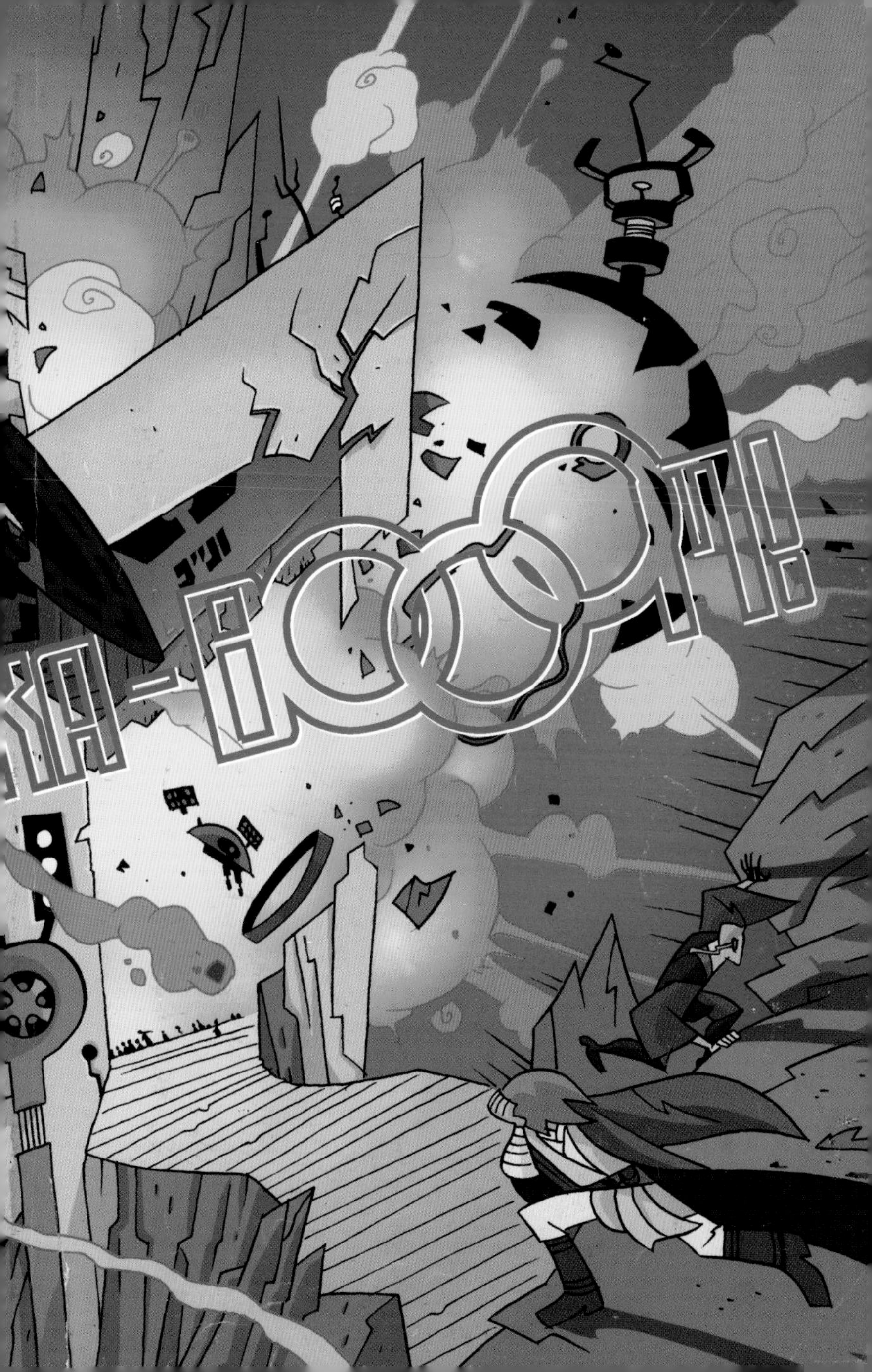
KA-BOOOM!

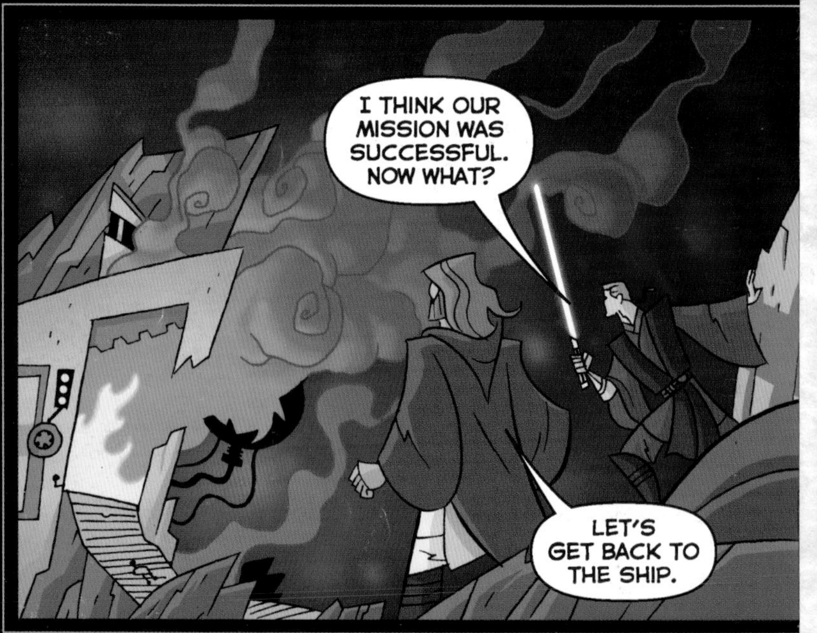
I THINK OUR MISSION WAS SUCCESSFUL. NOW WHAT?
LET'S GET BACK TO THE SHIP.

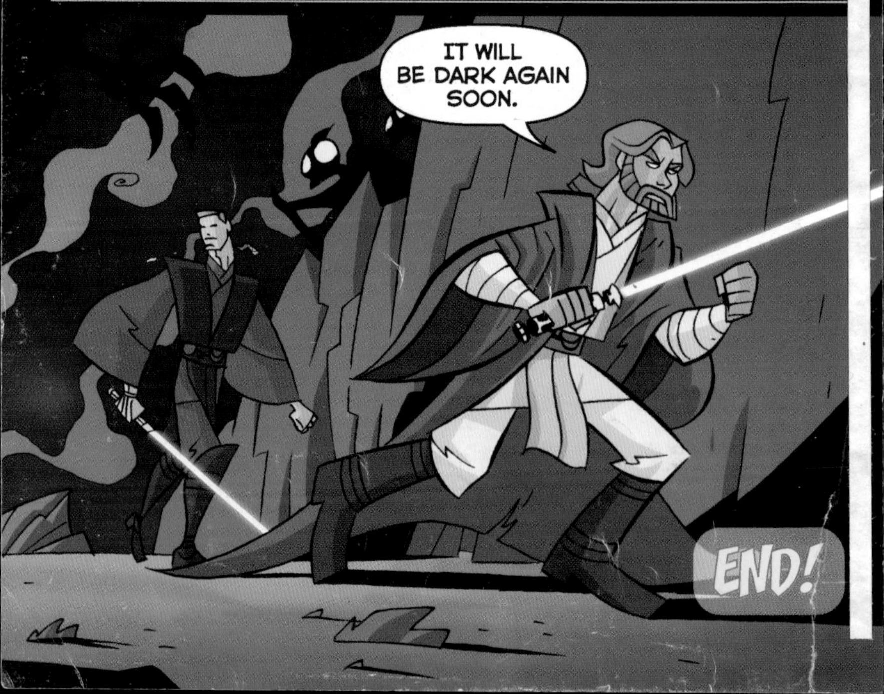
IT WILL BE DARK AGAIN SOON.
END!

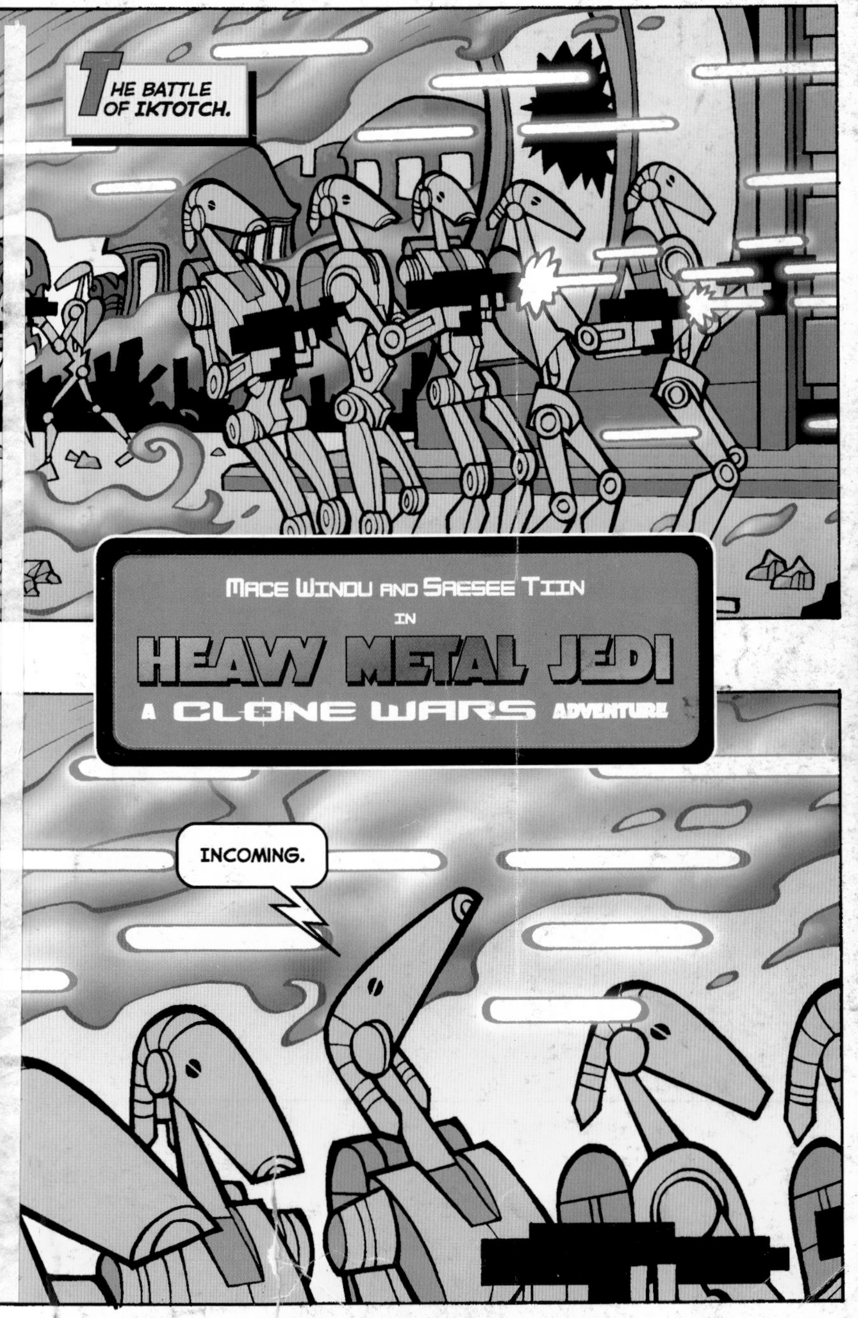
THE BATTLE OF IKTOTCH.
MACE WINDU AND SAESEE TIIN
IN
HEAVY METAL JEDI
A CLONE WARS ADVENTURE
INCOMING.

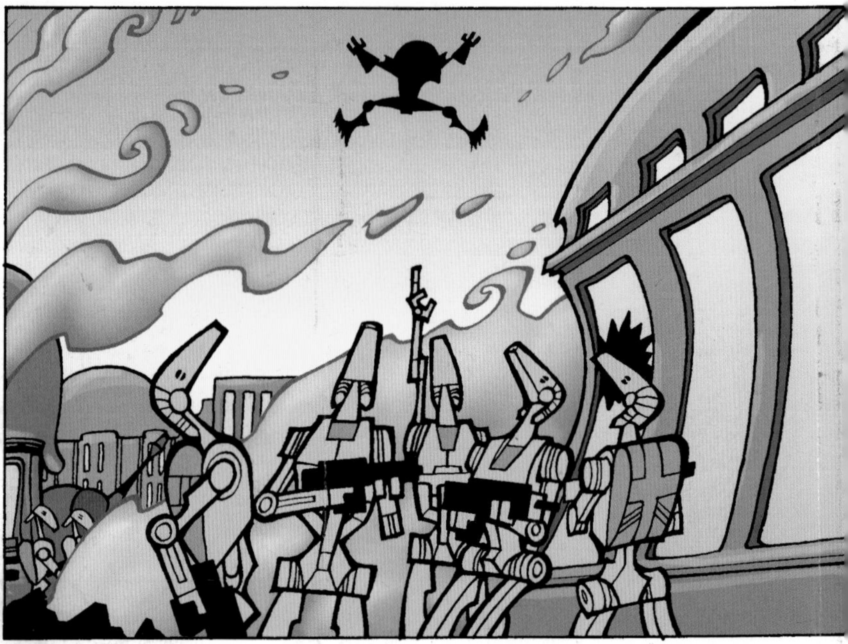

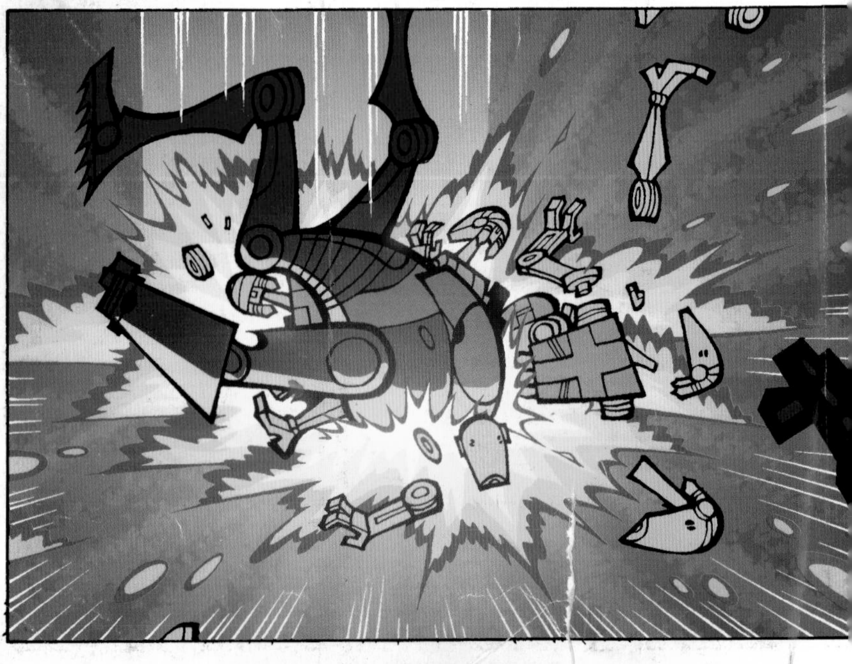

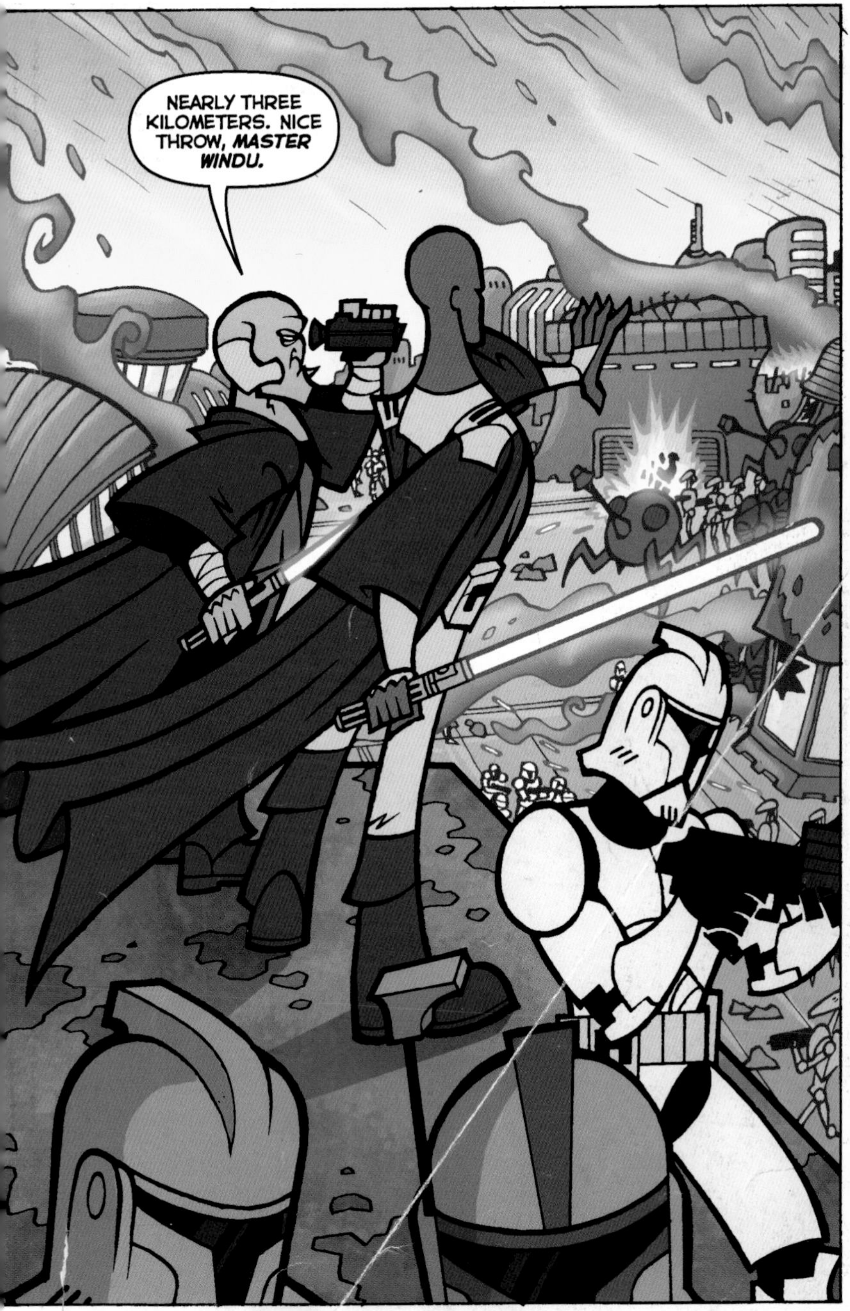
NEARLY THREE KILOMETERS. NICE THROW, MASTER WINDU.

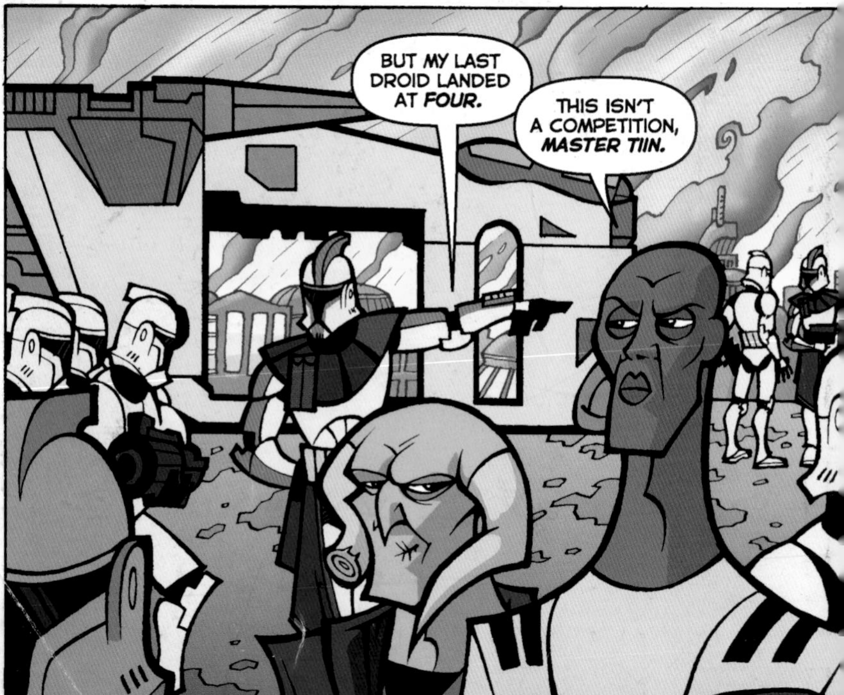
BUT MY LAST DROID LANDED AT FOUR.
THIS ISN'T A COMPETITION, MASTER TIIN.

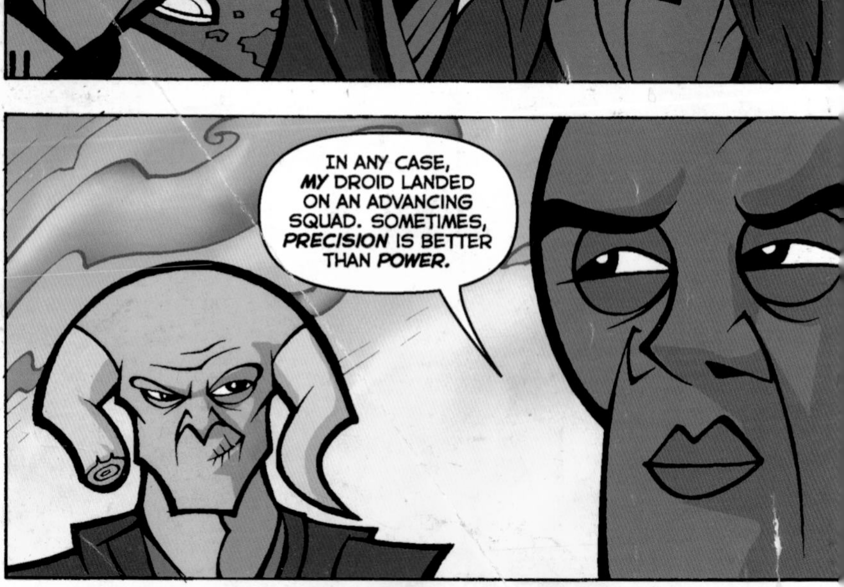
IN ANY CASE, MY DROID LANDED ON AN ADVANCING SQUAD. SOMETIMES, PRECISION IS BETTER THAN POWER.

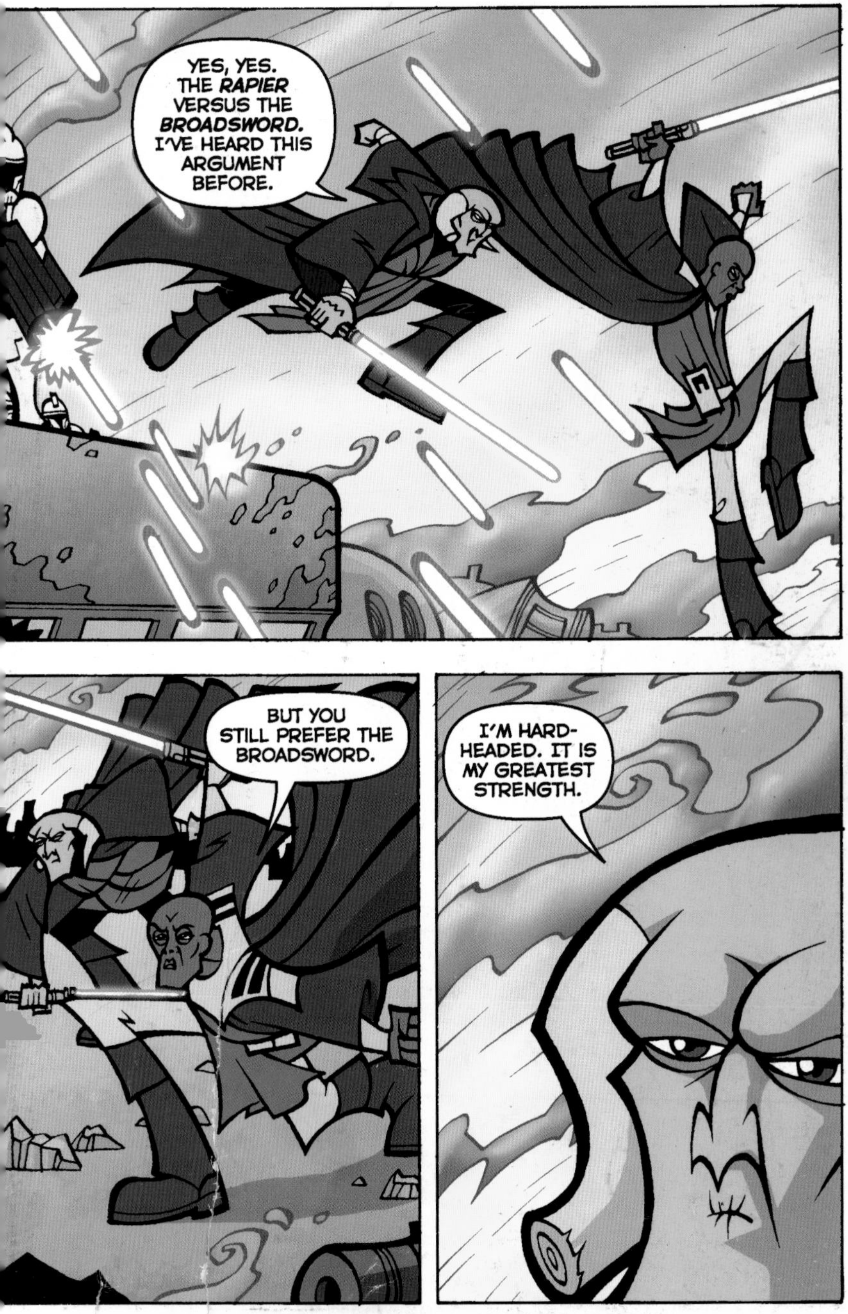
YES, YES. THE *RAPIER* VERSUS THE *BROADSWORD.* I'VE HEARD THIS ARGUMENT BEFORE.
BUT YOU STILL PREFER THE BROADSWORD.
I'M HARD-HEADED. IT IS MY GREATEST STRENGTH.

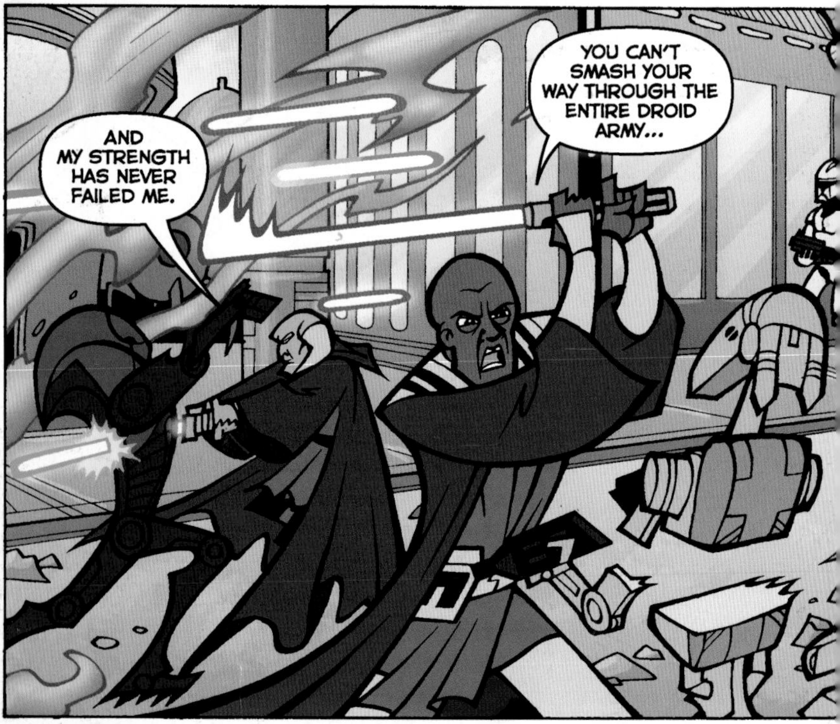
AND MY STRENGTH HAS NEVER FAILED ME.
YOU CAN'T SMASH YOUR WAY THROUGH THE ENTIRE DROID ARMY...

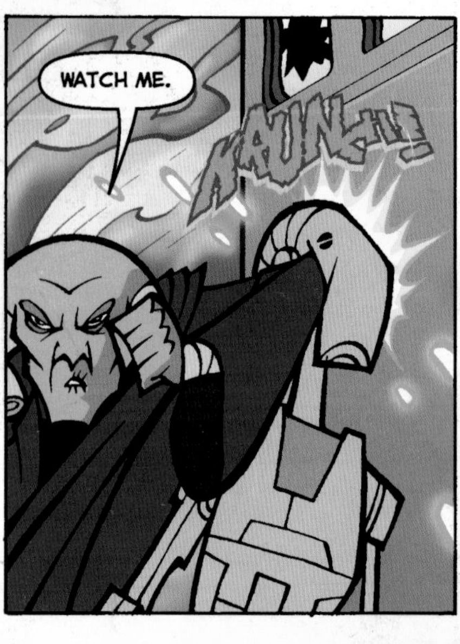
WATCH ME.

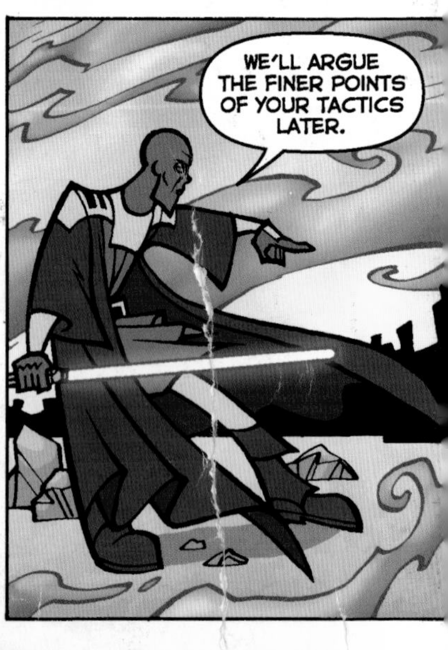
WE'LL ARGUE THE FINER POINTS OF YOUR TACTICS LATER.

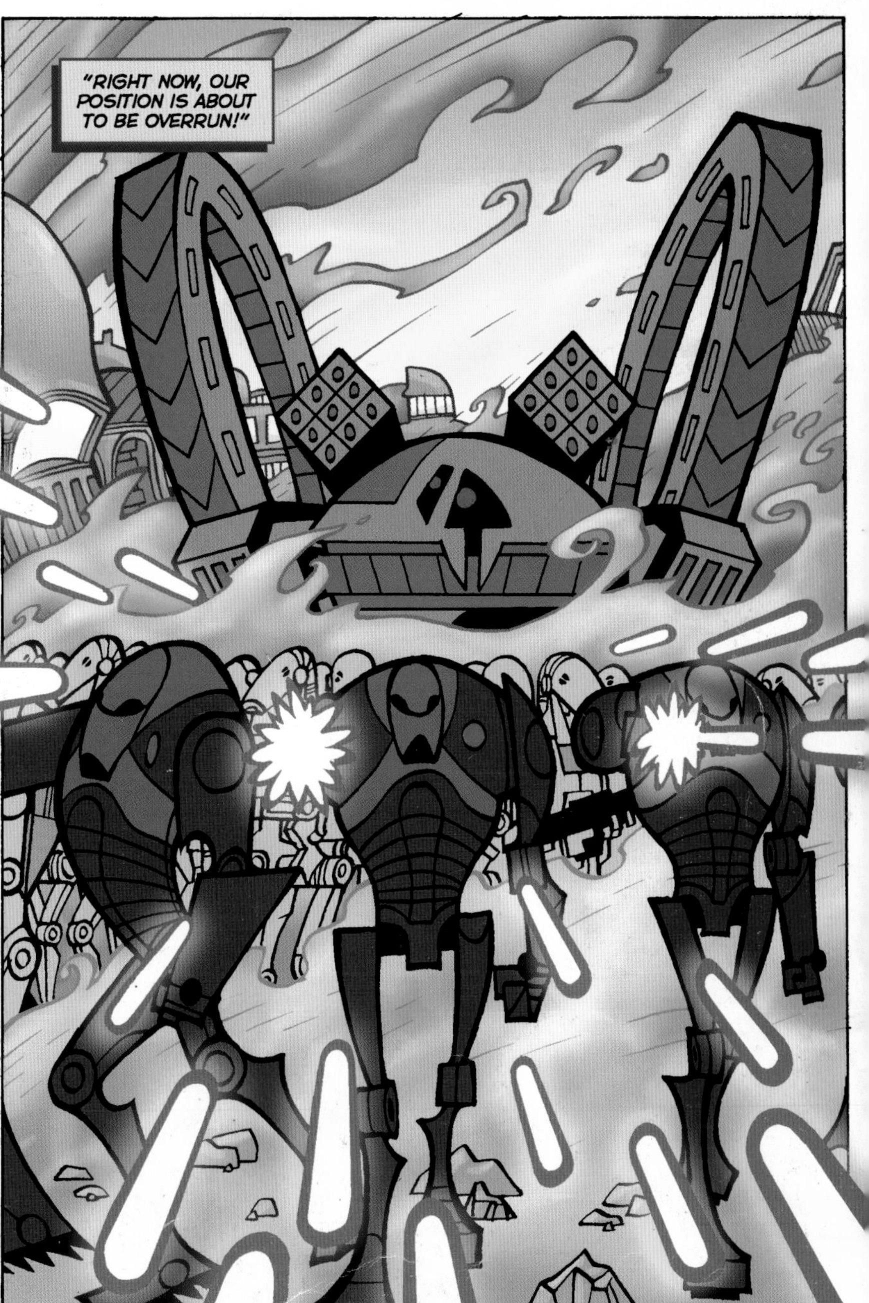
"RIGHT NOW, OUR POSITION IS ABOUT TO BE OVERRUN!"

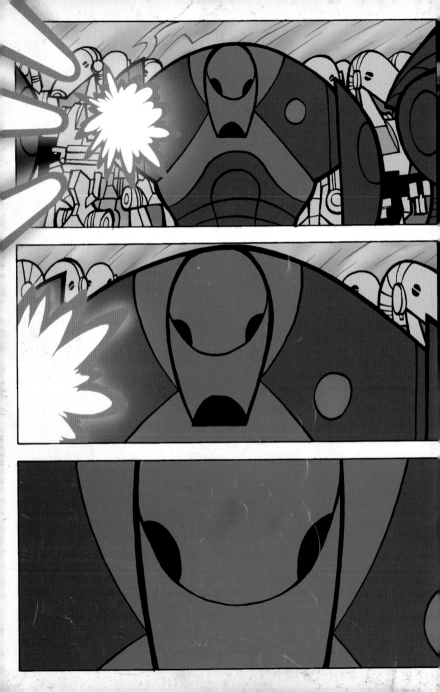

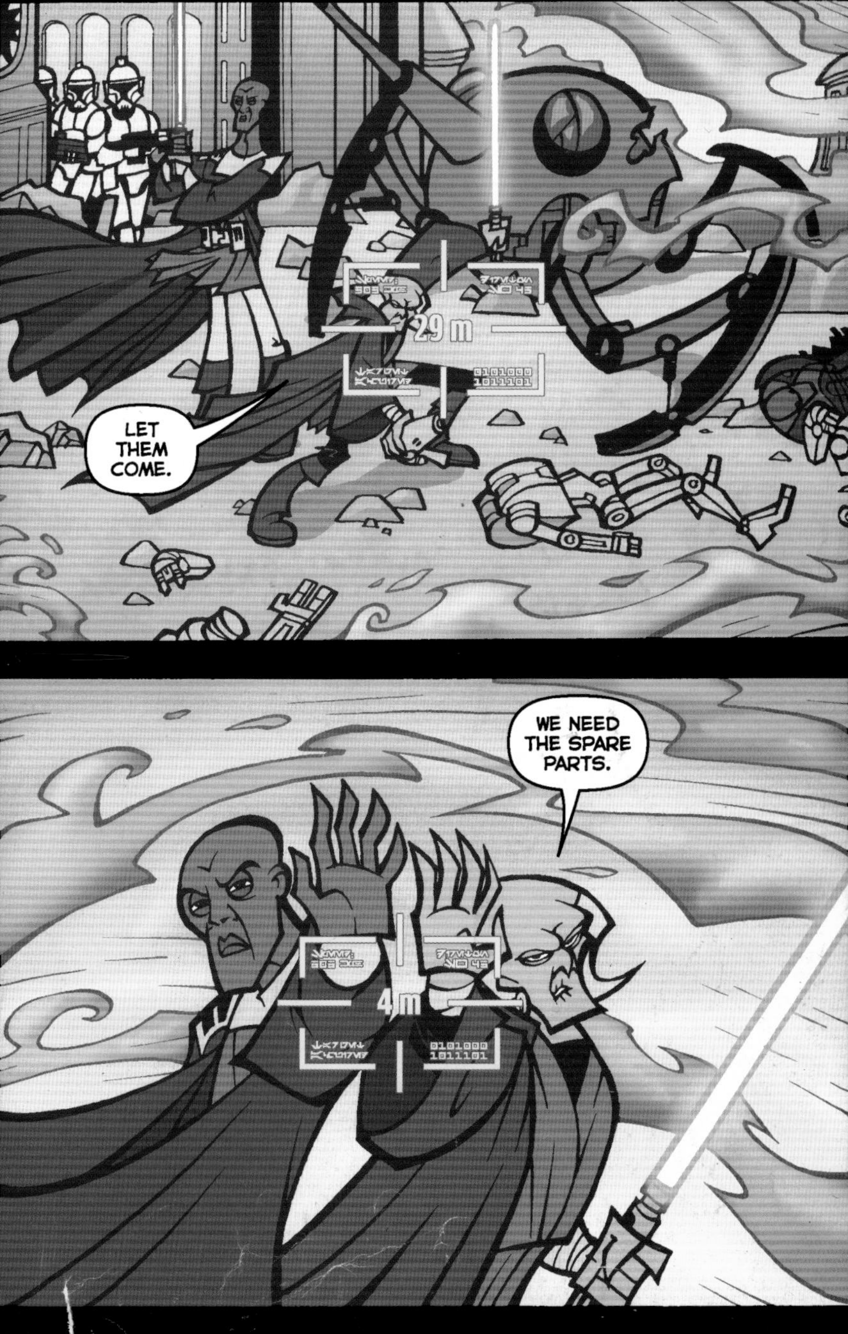
29 m
0101000
1011101
LET THEM COME.
WE NEED THE SPARE PARTS.
4 m
0101000
1011101

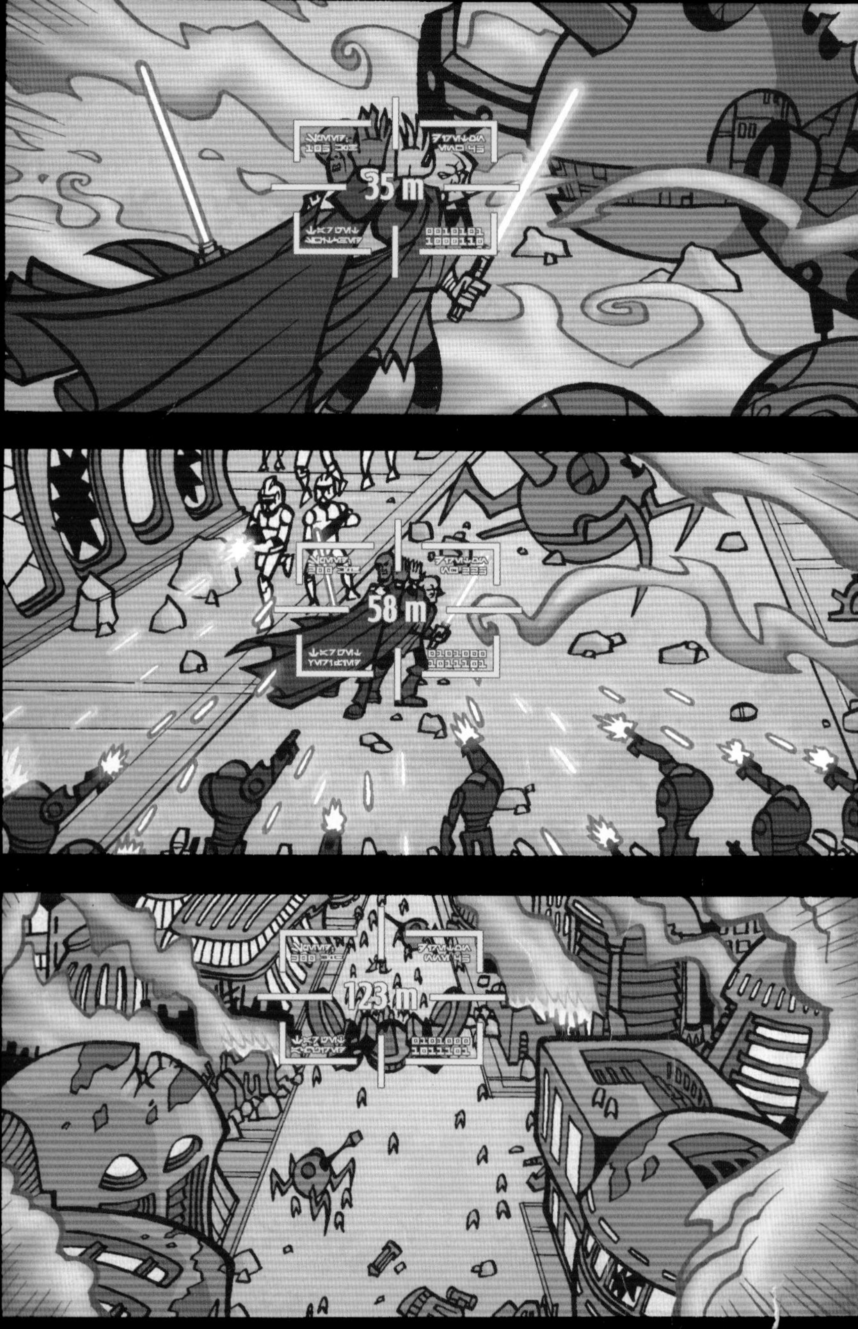
35 m
0010101
1000110
58 m
123 m
0101000
1011101

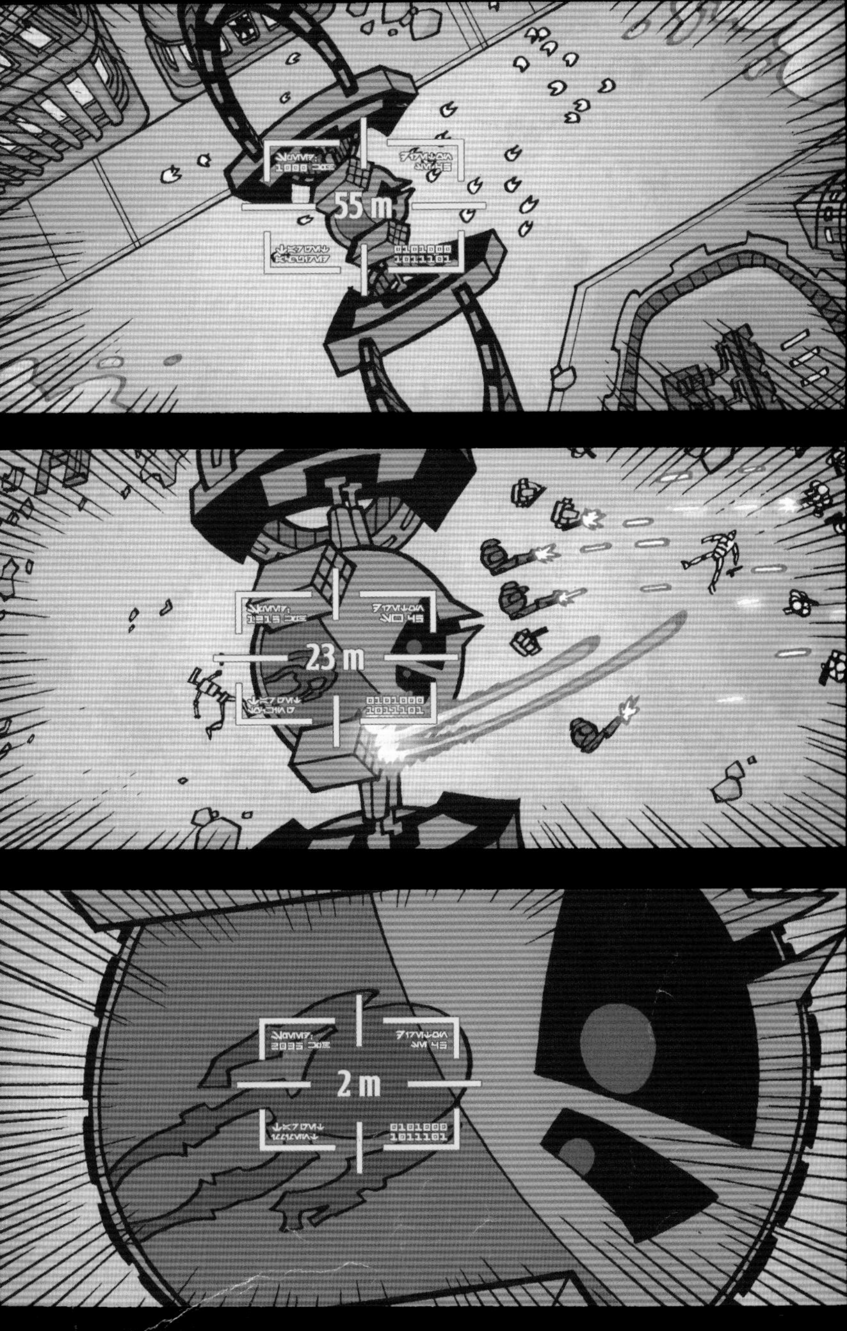
55 m
0101000
1011101
23 m
0101000
1011101
2 m
0101000
1011101

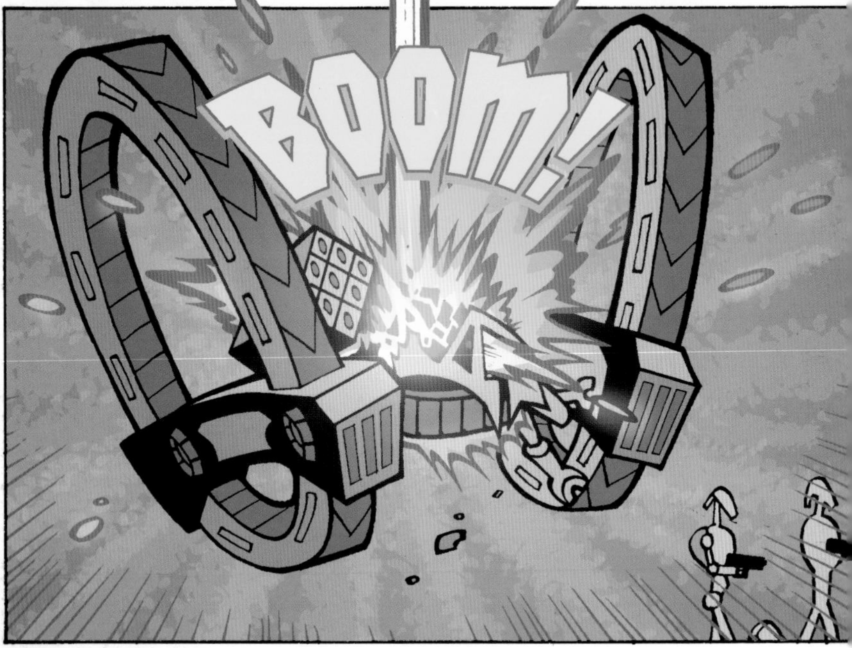
BOOM!

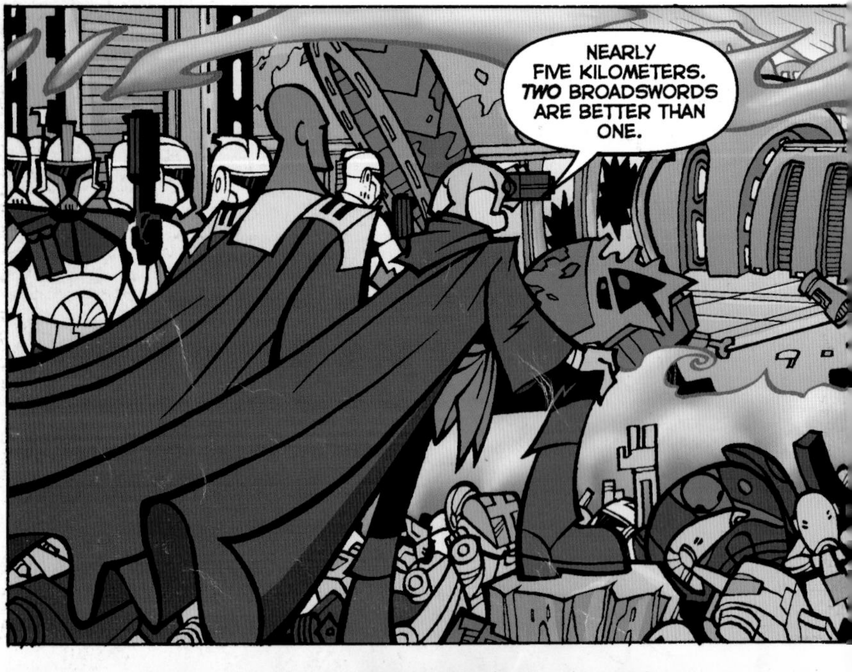
NEARLY FIVE KILOMETERS. *TWO* BROADSWORDS ARE BETTER THAN ONE.

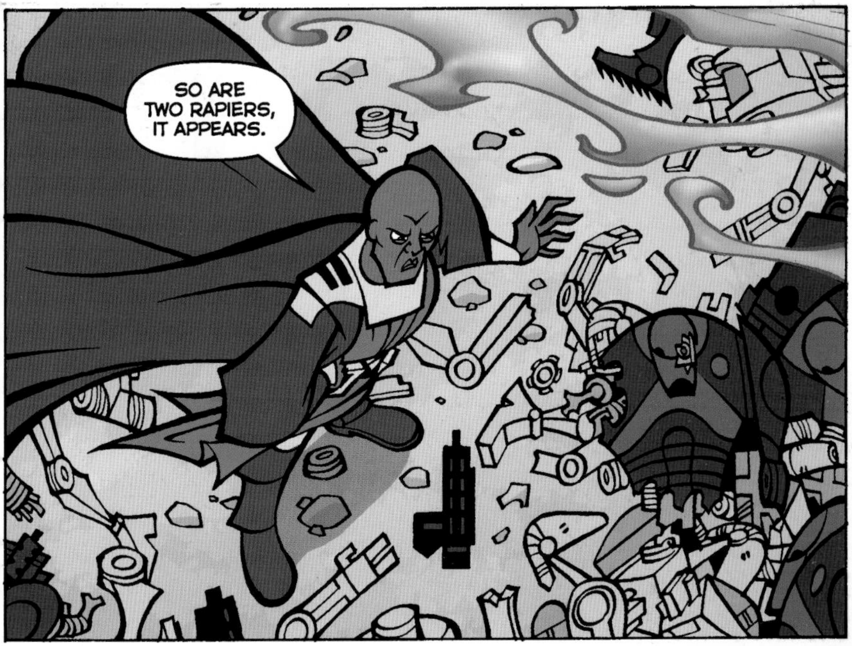
SO ARE TWO RAPIERS, IT APPEARS.

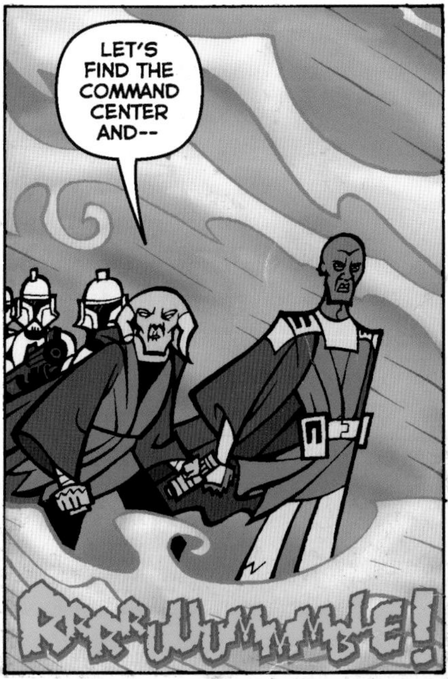
LET'S FIND THE COMMAND CENTER AND--
RRRRUUMMMBLE!

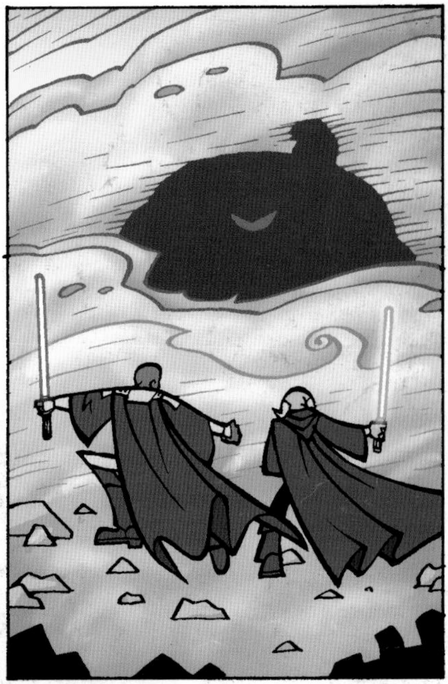

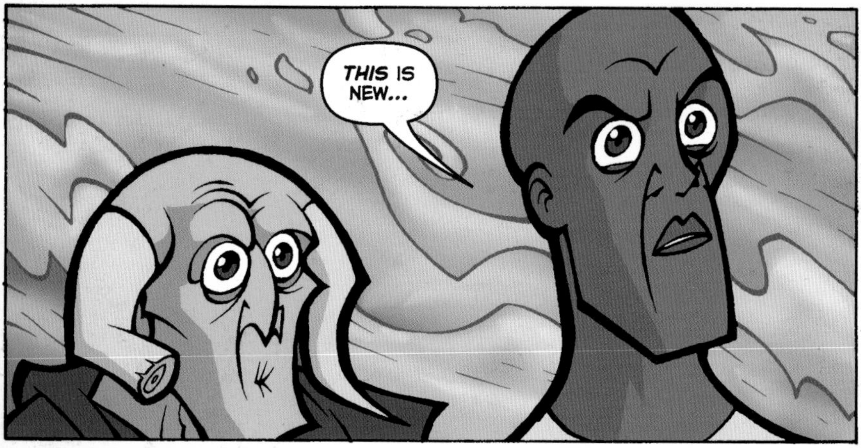
THIS IS NEW...

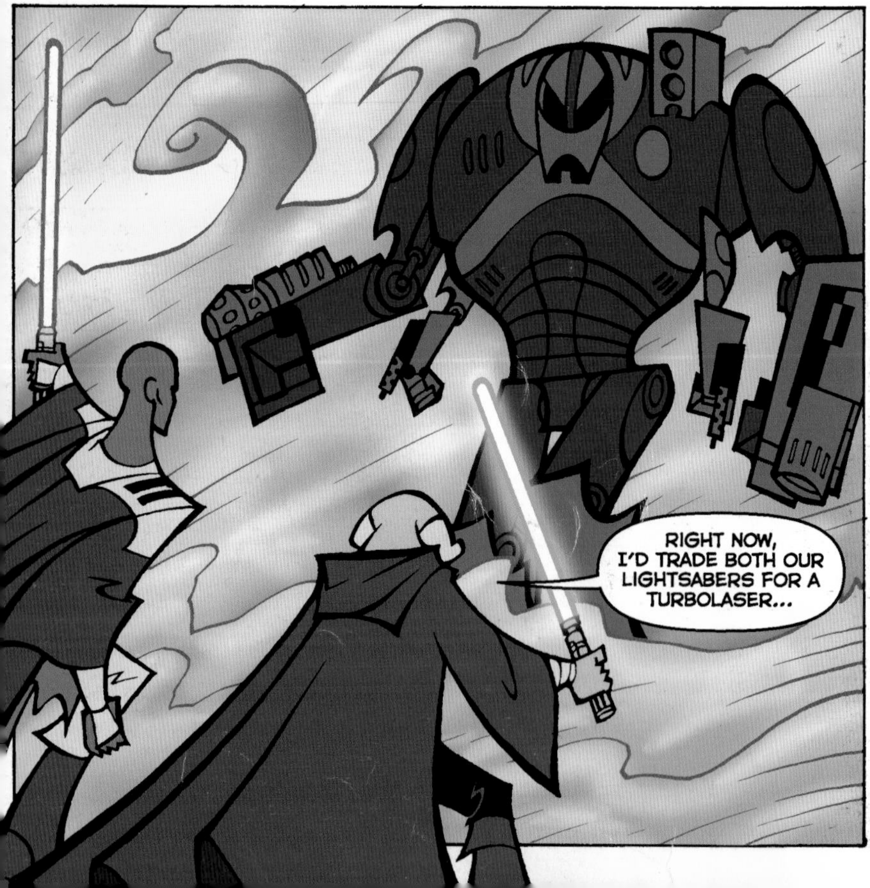
RIGHT NOW, I'D TRADE BOTH OUR LIGHTSABERS FOR A TURBOLASER...

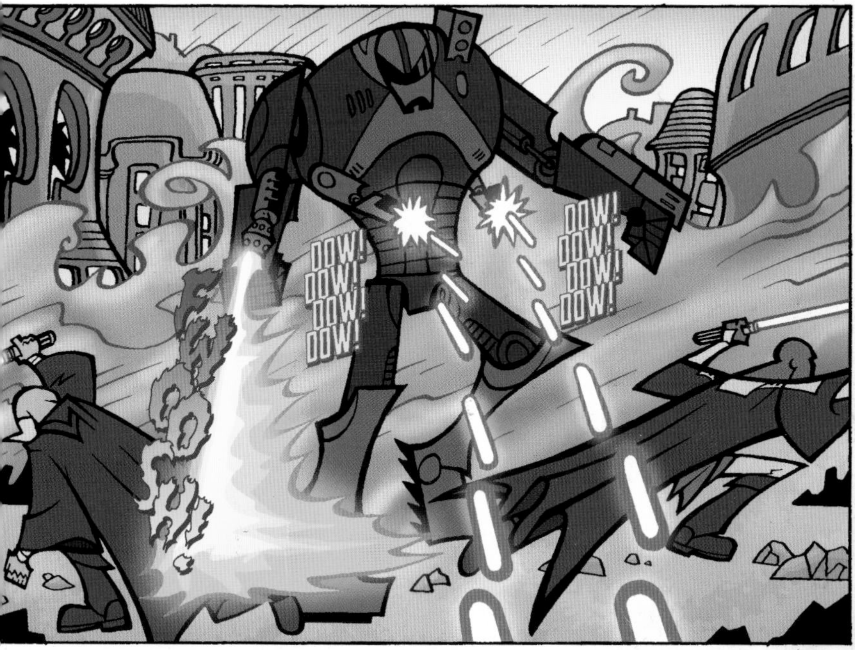
DOW!
DOW!
DOW!
DOW!
DOW!
DOW!
DOW!
DOW!

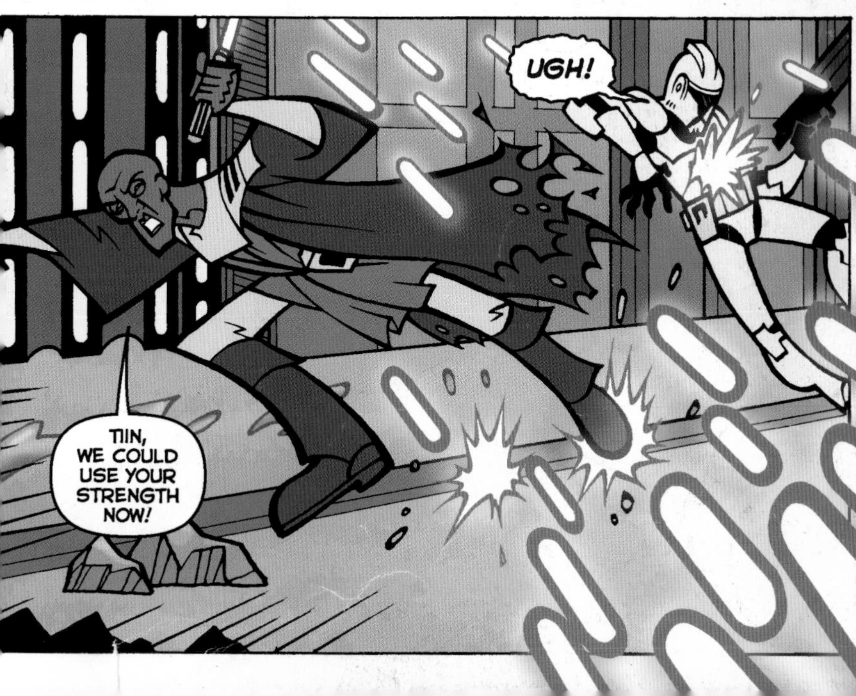
UGH!
TIIN,
WE COULD
USE YOUR
STRENGTH
NOW!

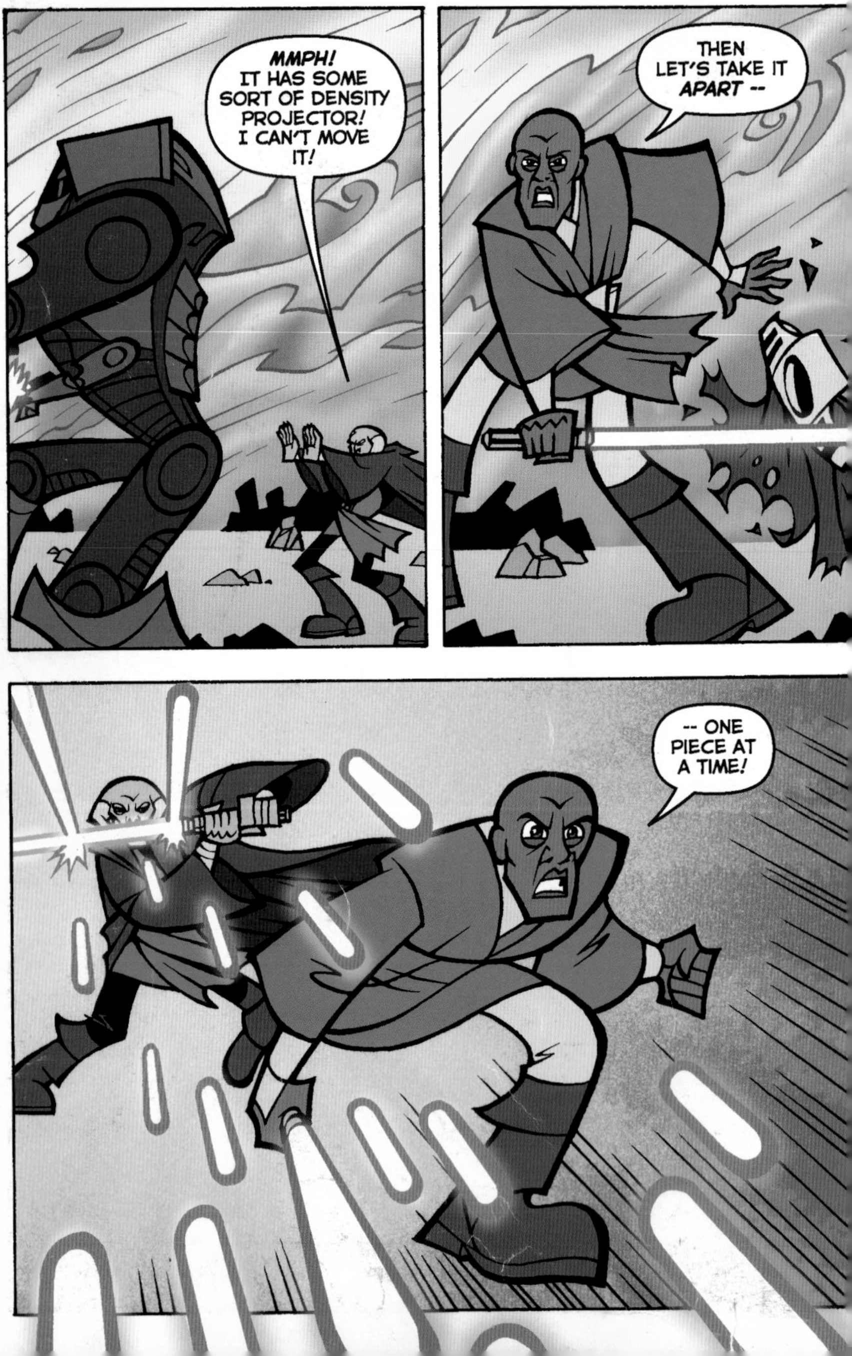
MMPH! IT HAS SOME SORT OF DENSITY PROJECTOR! I CAN'T MOVE IT!
THEN LET'S TAKE IT APART --
-- ONE PIECE AT A TIME!

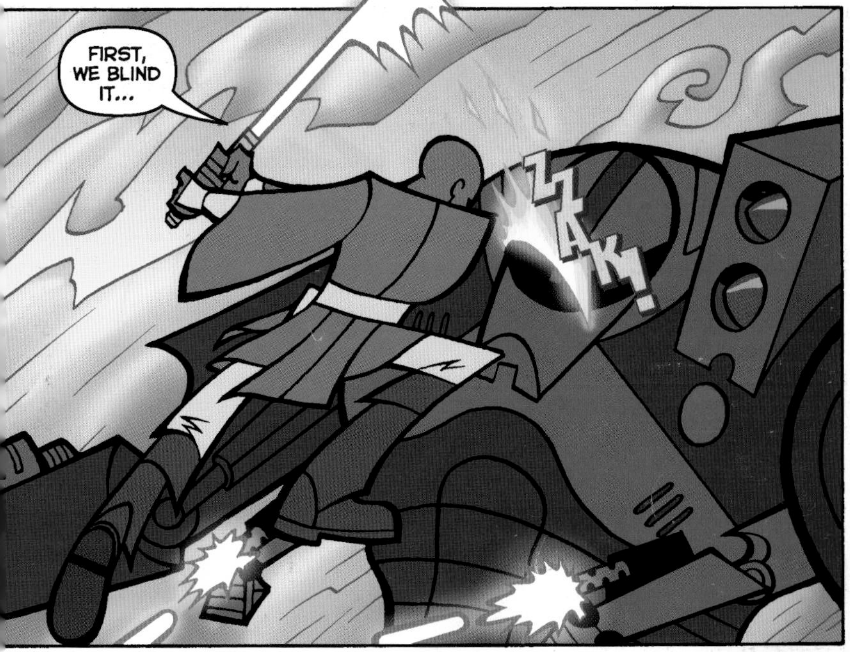
FIRST, WE BLIND IT...
ZZAK!

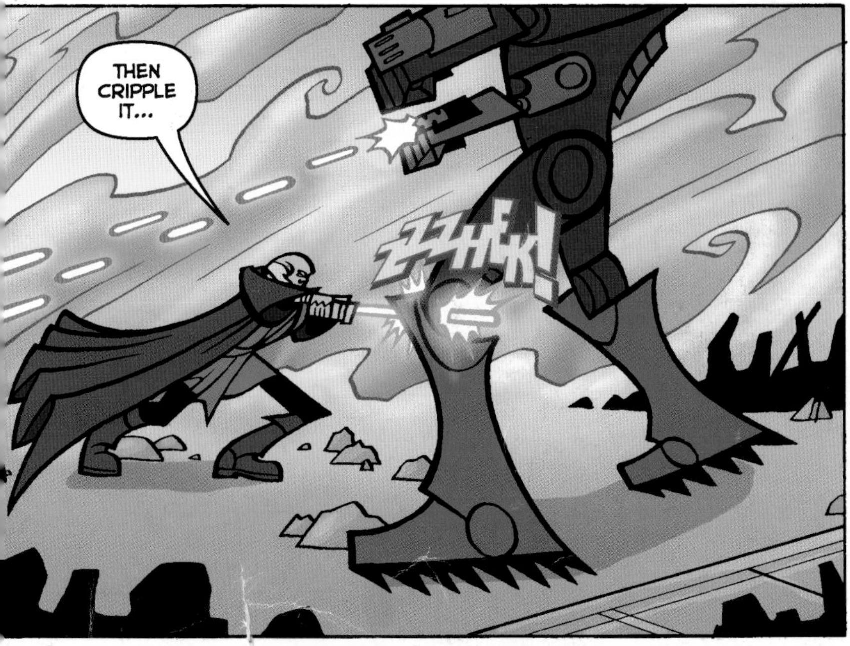
THEN CRIPPLE IT...

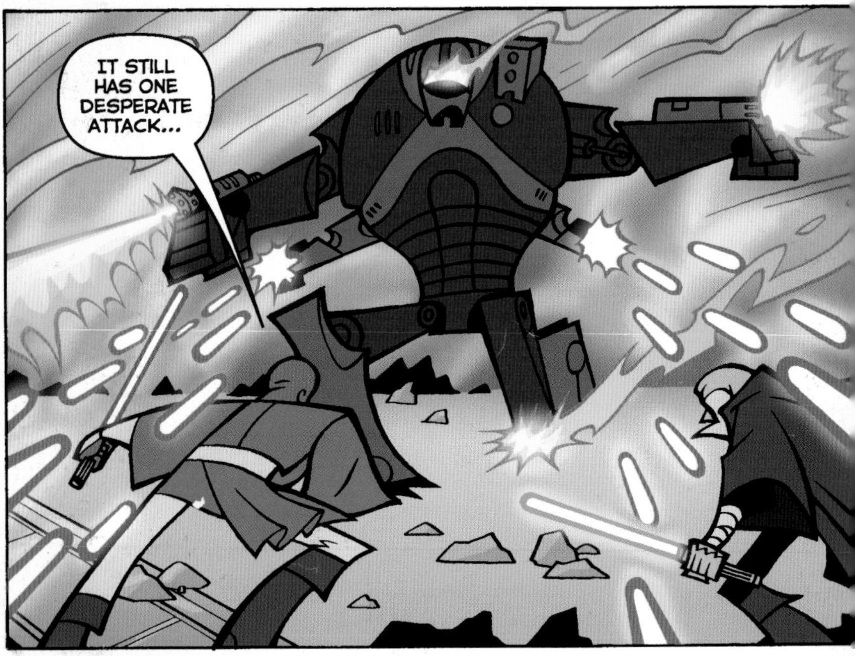
IT STILL HAS ONE DESPERATE ATTACK...

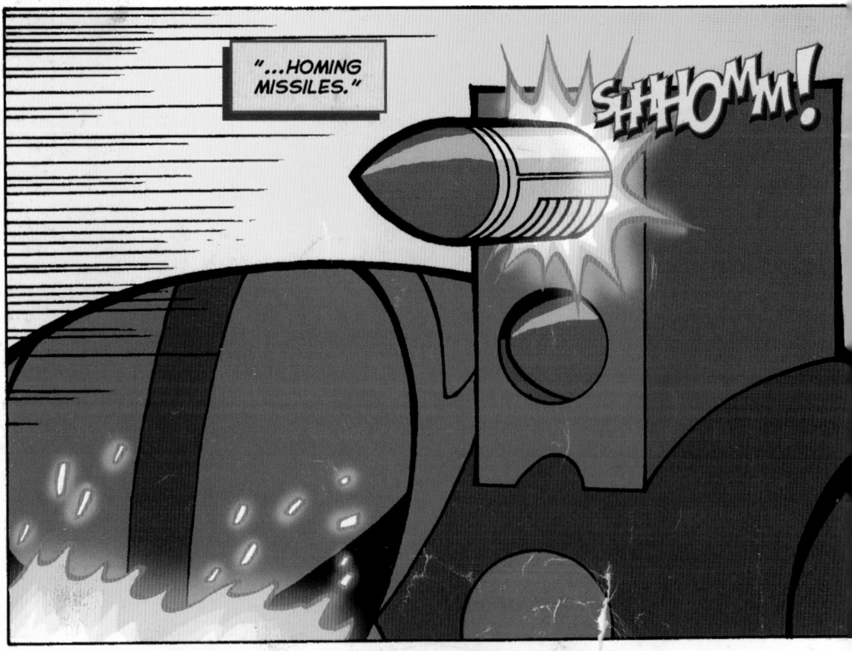
"...HOMING MISSILES."
SHHOMM!

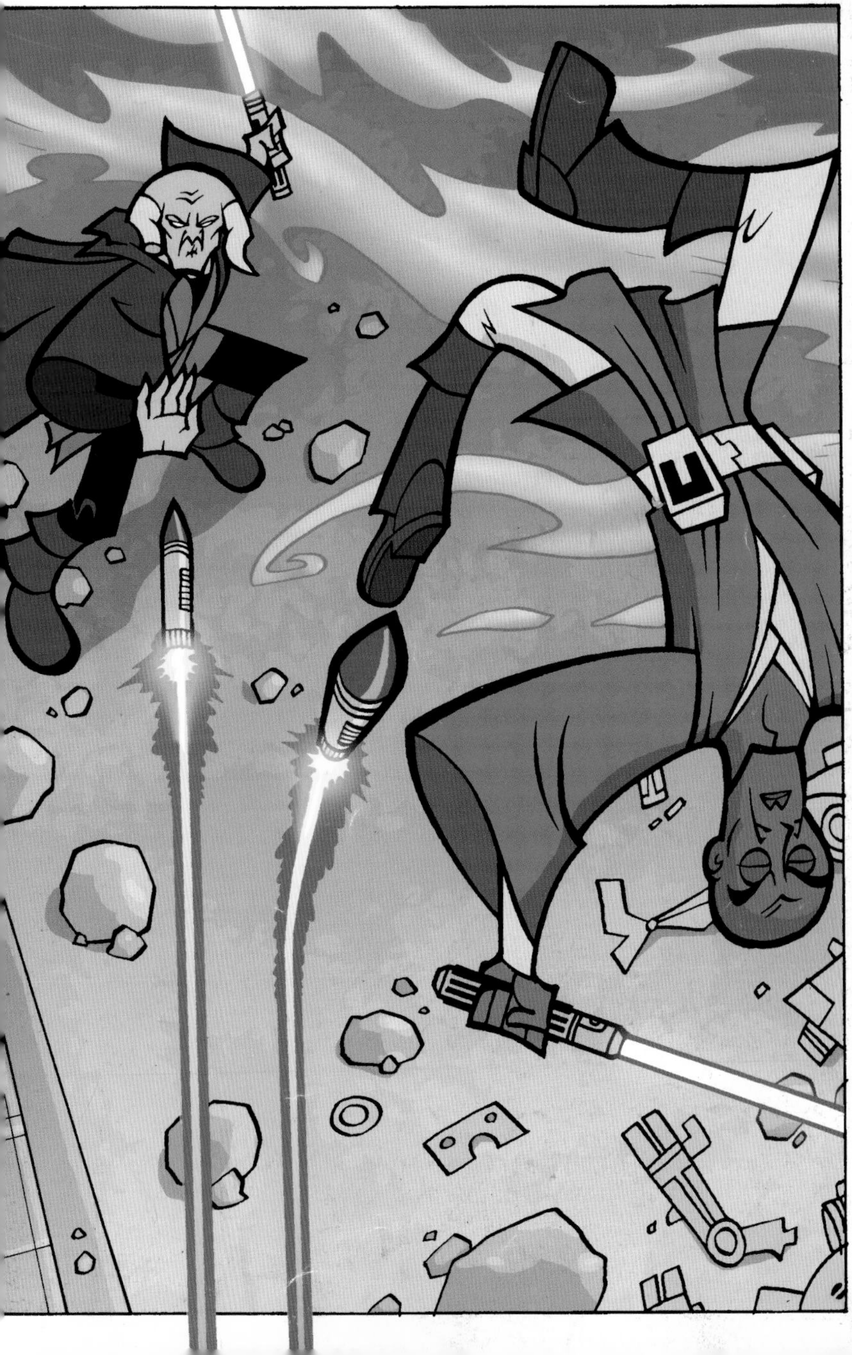

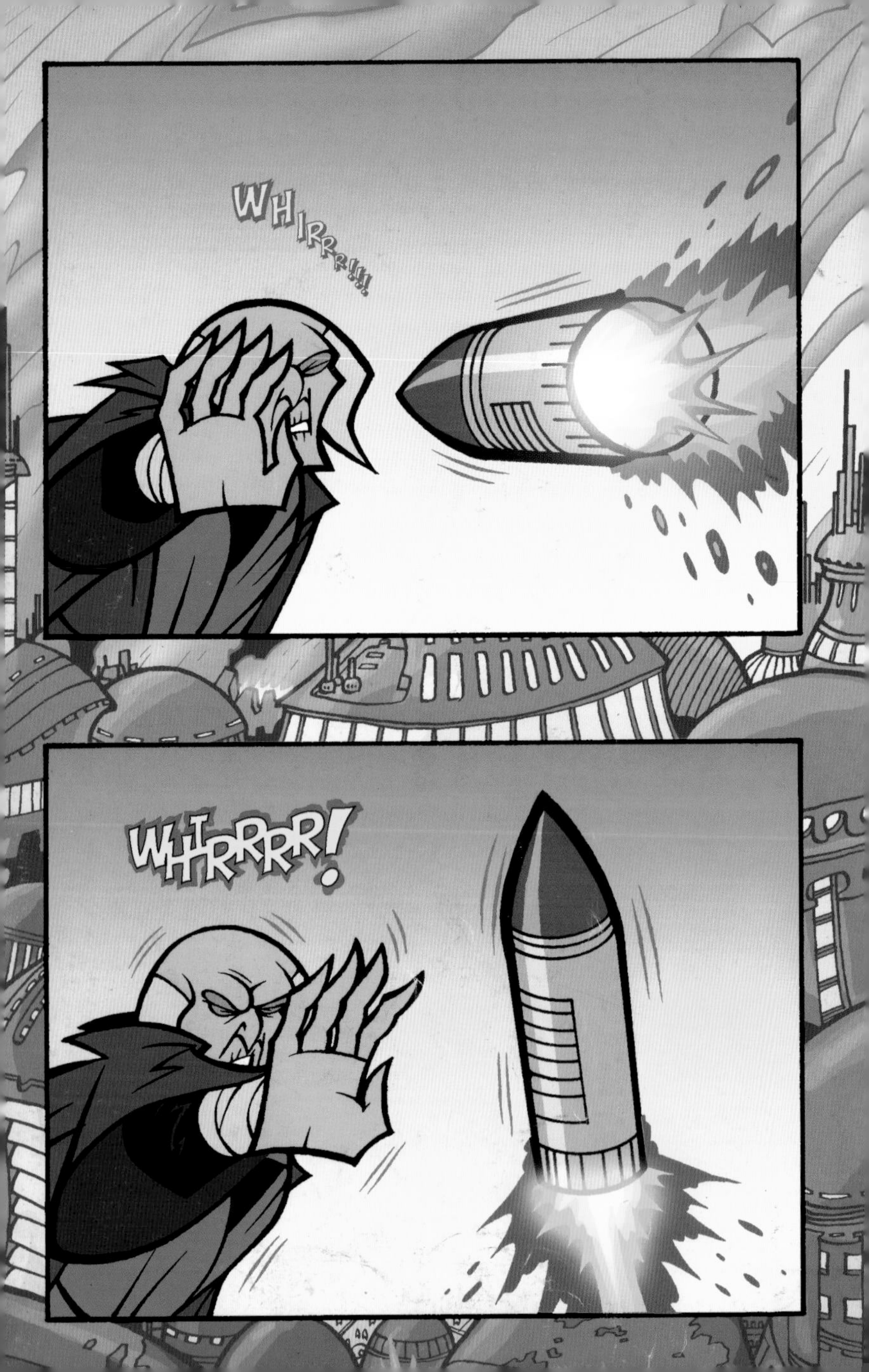
WHIRRR!!!!
WHIRRRR!

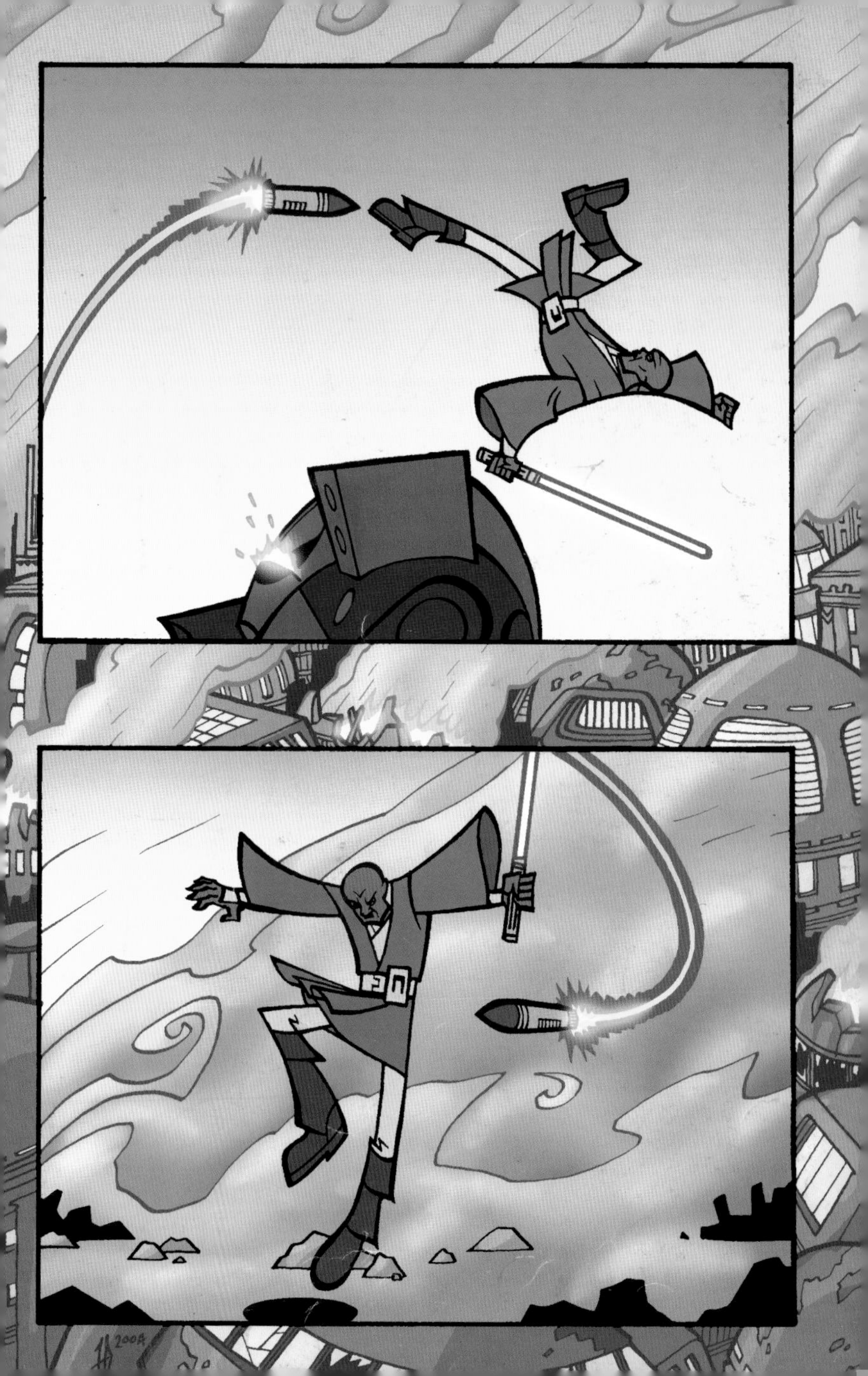

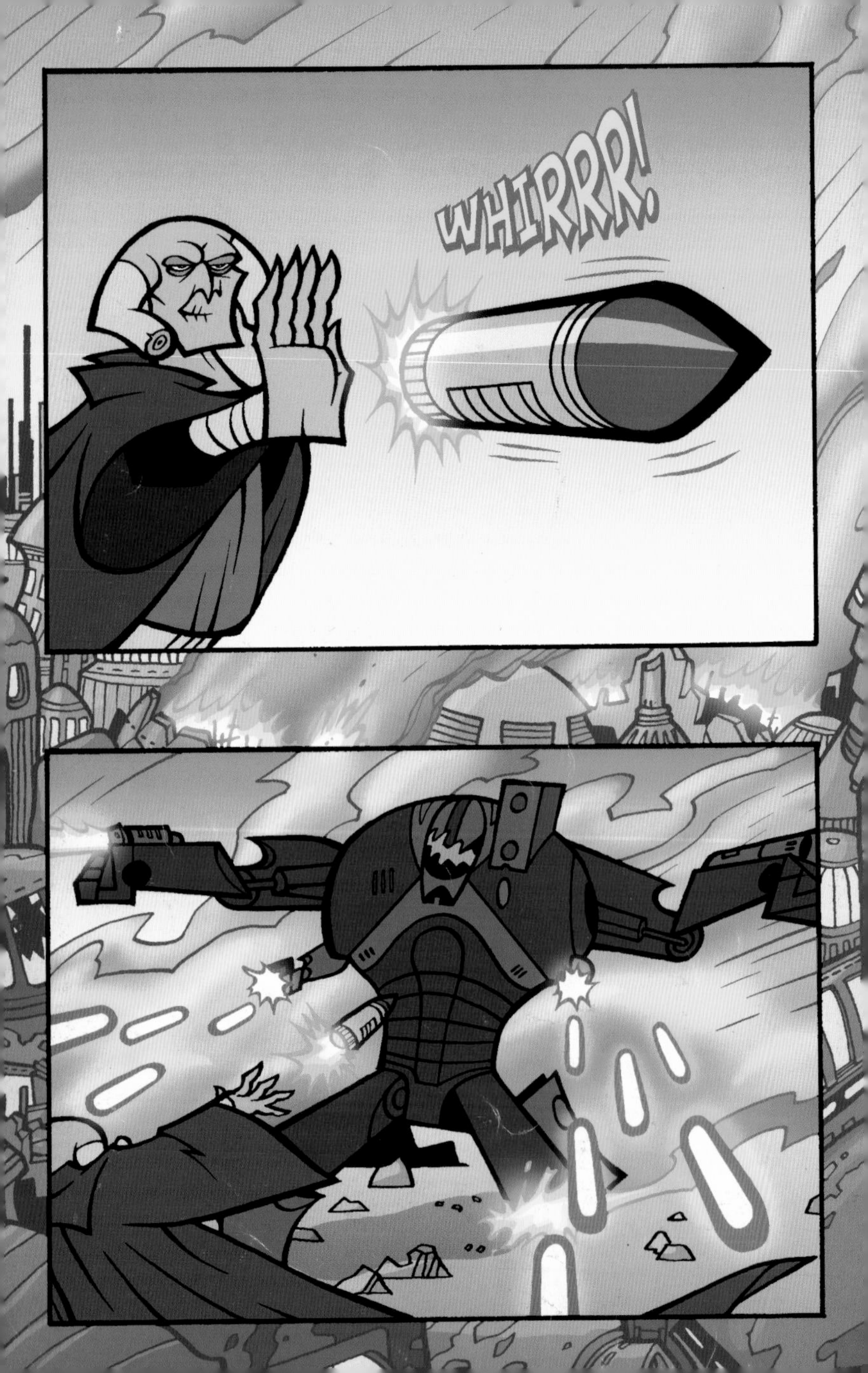
WHIRRR!

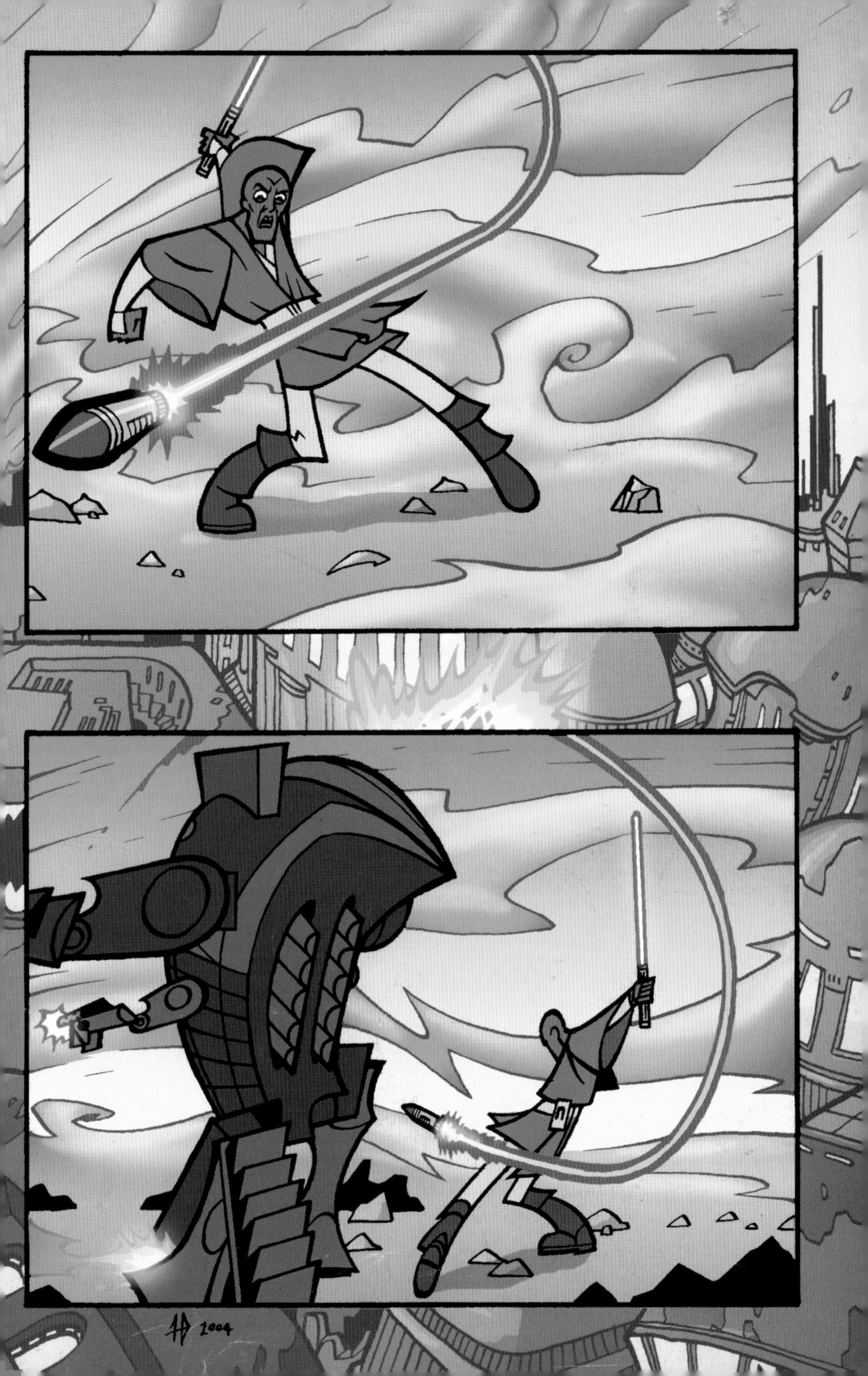
2004

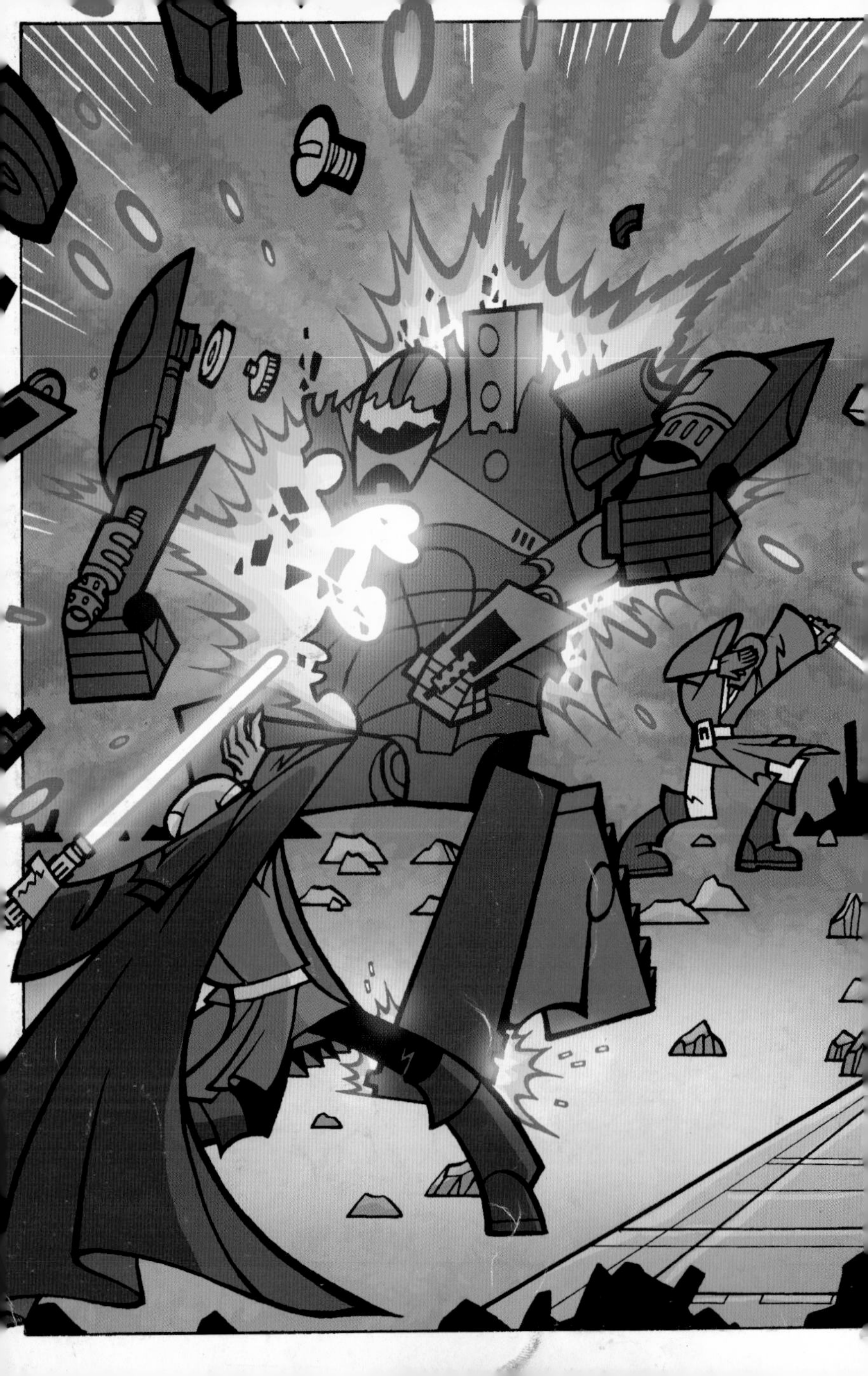

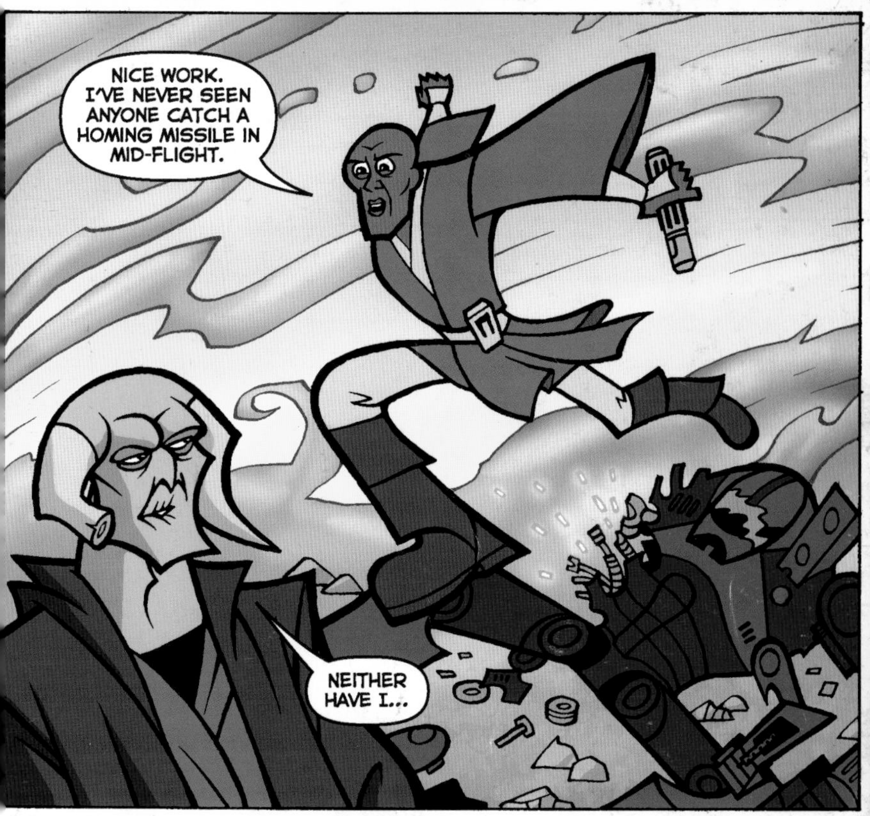
NICE WORK. I'VE NEVER SEEN ANYONE CATCH A HOMING MISSILE IN MID-FLIGHT.
NEITHER HAVE I...

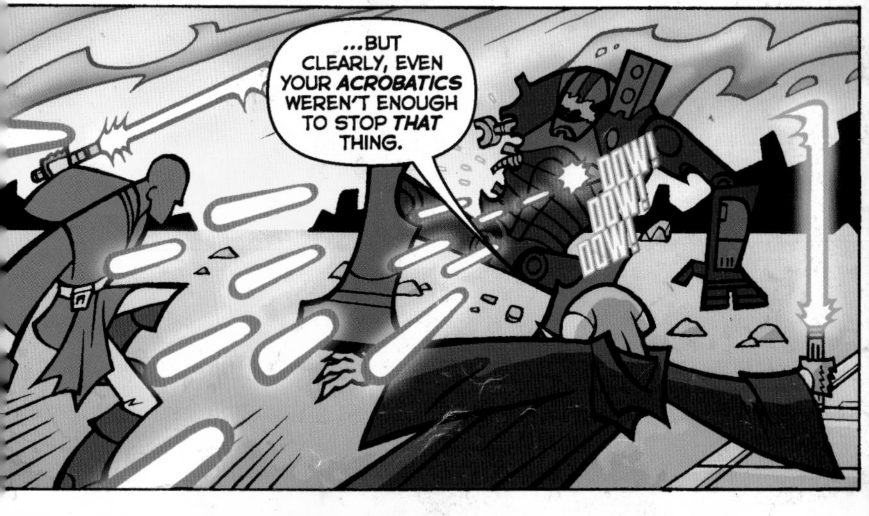
...BUT CLEARLY, EVEN YOUR *ACROBATICS* WEREN'T ENOUGH TO STOP *THAT* THING.
DOW! DOW! DOW!

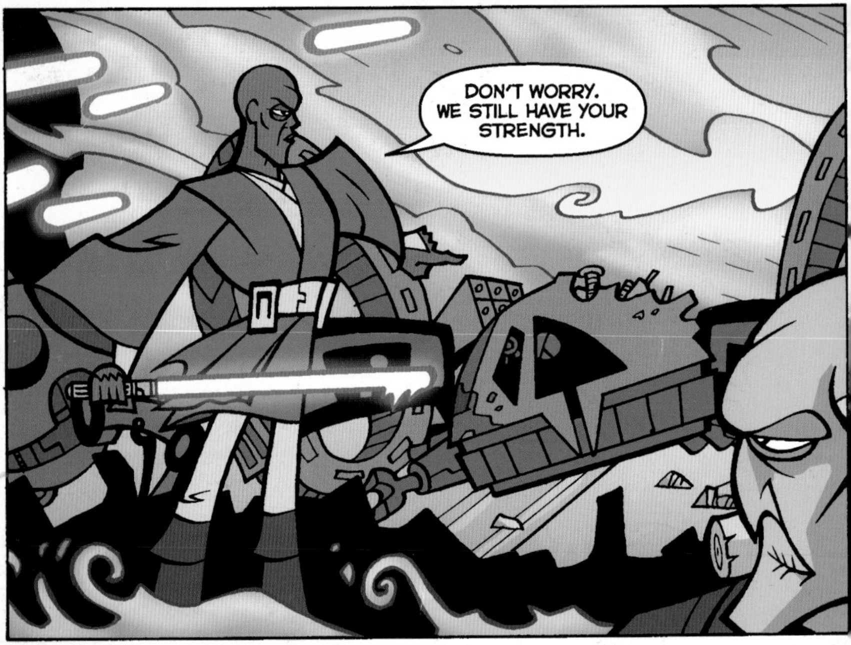
DON'T WORRY. WE STILL HAVE YOUR STRENGTH.

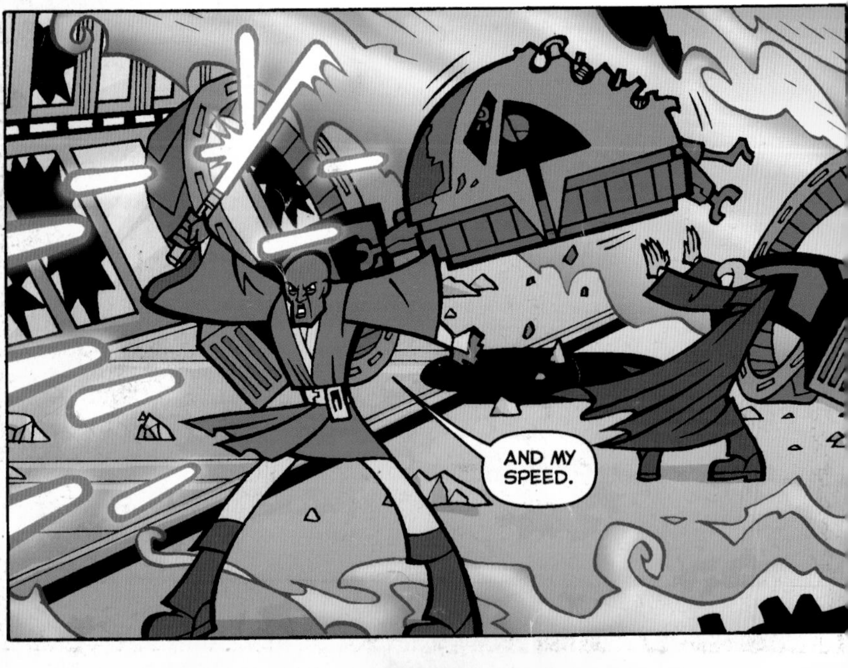
AND MY SPEED.

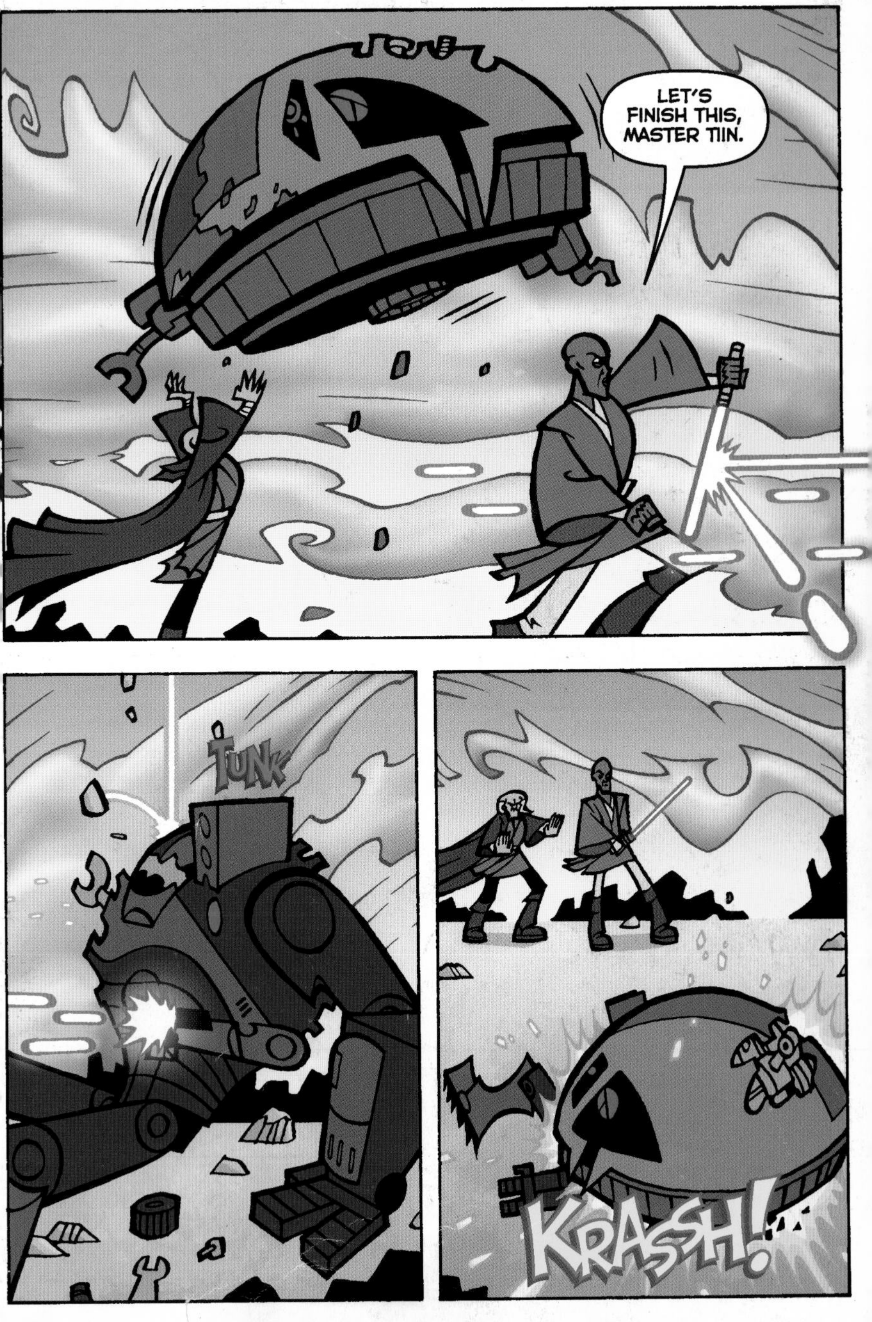
LET'S FINISH THIS, MASTER TIIN.
TUNK
KRASH!

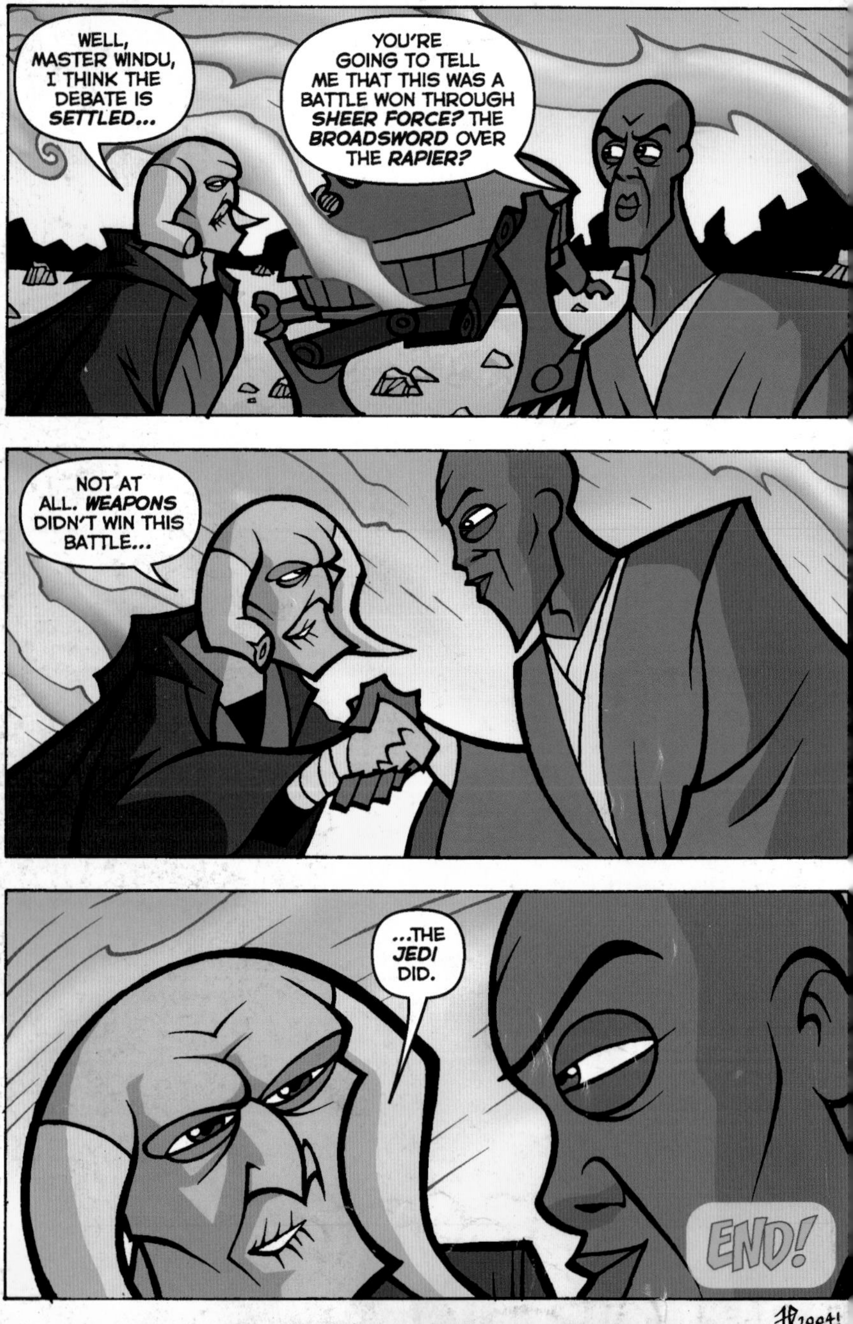
WELL, MASTER WINDU, I THINK THE DEBATE IS *SETTLED...*
YOU'RE GOING TO TELL ME THAT THIS WAS A BATTLE WON THROUGH *SHEER FORCE?* THE *BROADSWORD* OVER THE *RAPIER?*
NOT AT ALL. *WEAPONS* DIDN'T WIN THIS BATTLE...
...THE *JEDI* DID.
END!
2004!

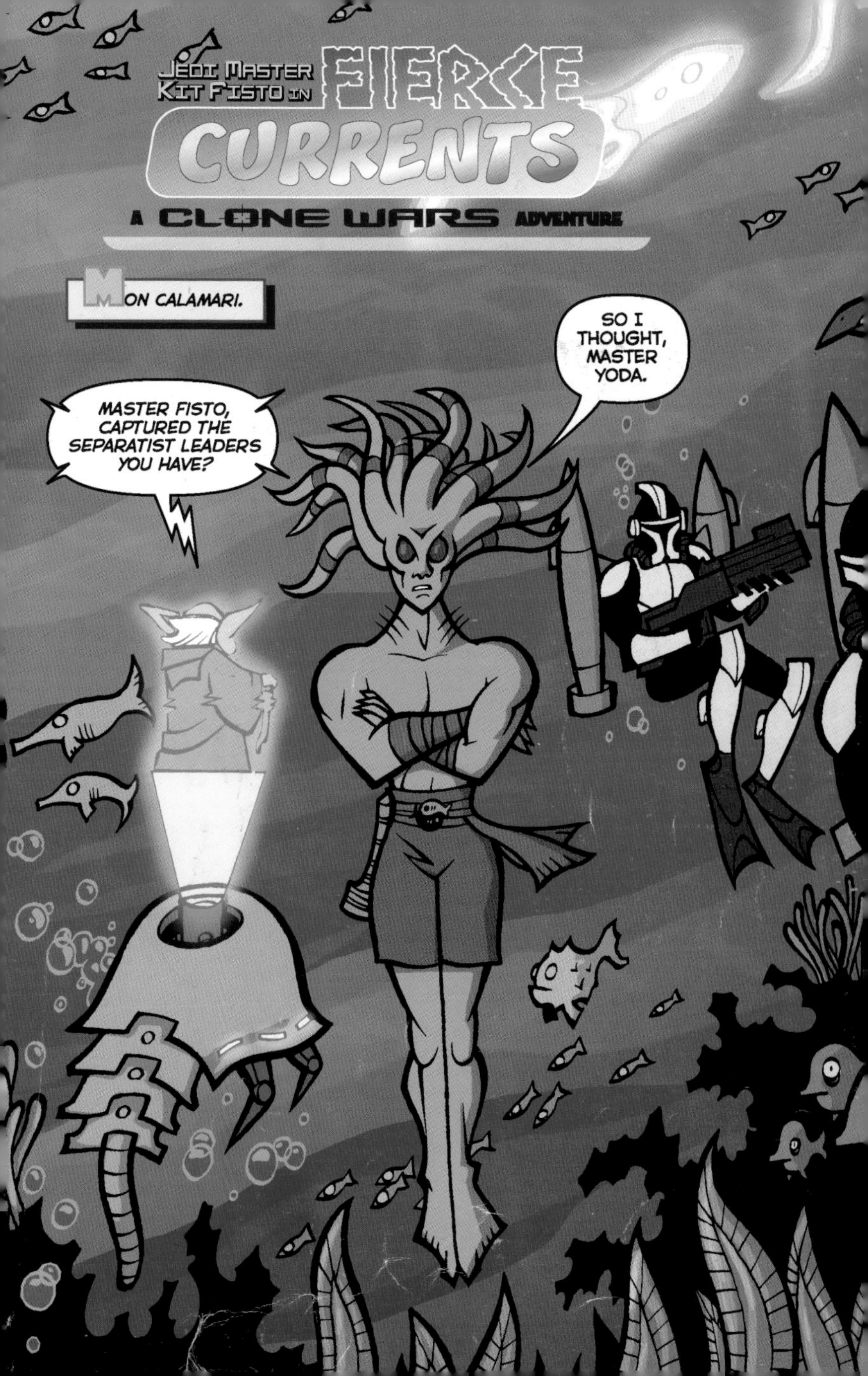
JEDI MASTER KIT FISTO IN
FIERCE CURRENTS
A CLONE WARS ADVENTURE
MON CALAMARI.
MASTER FISTO, CAPTURED THE SEPARATIST LEADERS YOU HAVE?
SO I THOUGHT, MASTER YODA.

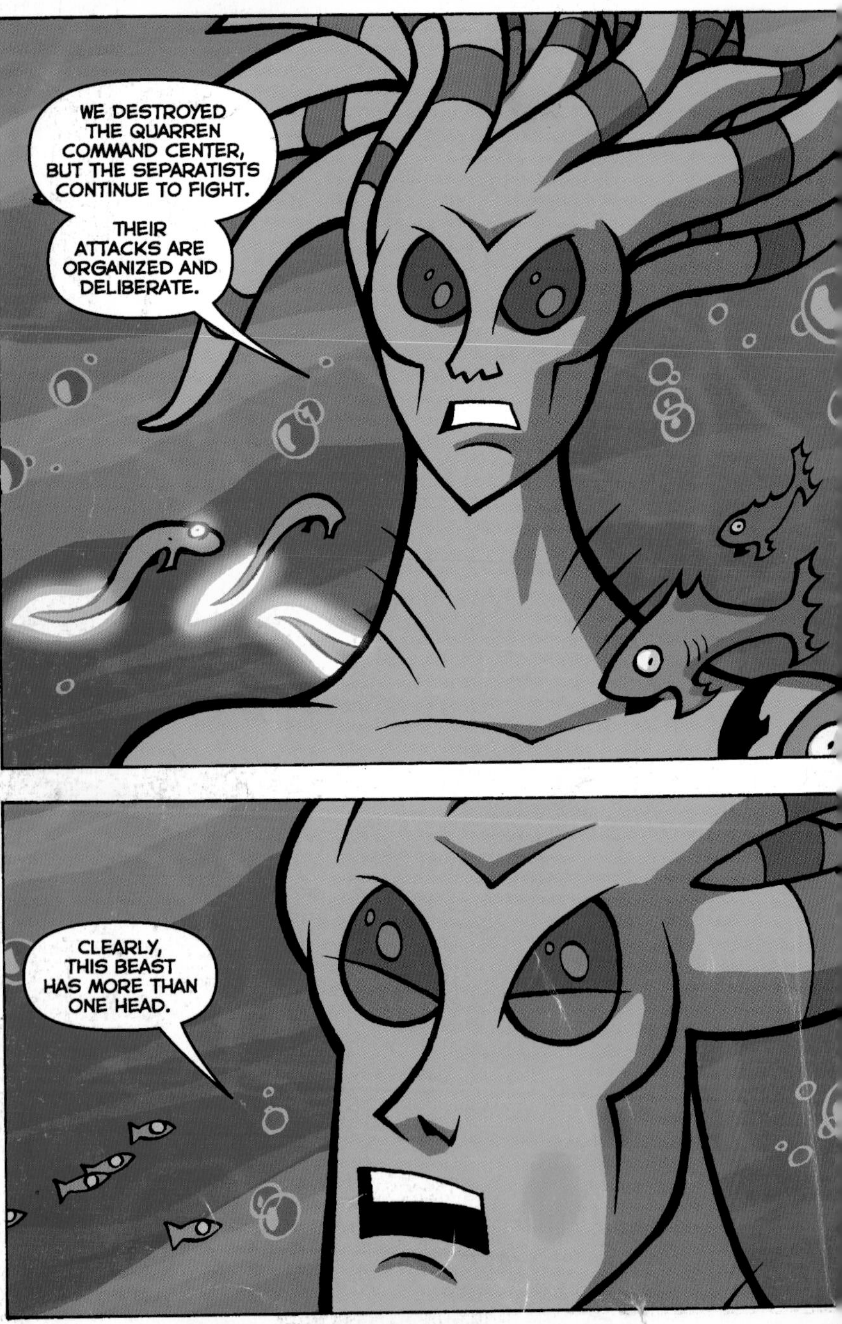
WE DESTROYED THE QUARREN COMMAND CENTER, BUT THE SEPARATISTS CONTINUE TO FIGHT.
THEIR ATTACKS ARE ORGANIZED AND DELIBERATE.
CLEARLY, THIS BEAST HAS MORE THAN ONE HEAD.

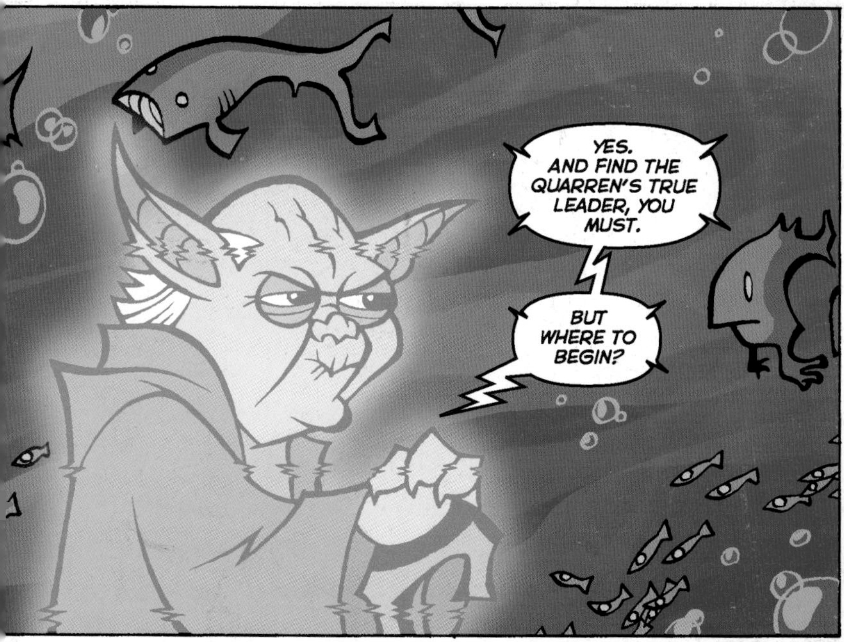
YES. AND FIND THE QUARREN'S TRUE LEADER, YOU MUST.
BUT WHERE TO BEGIN?

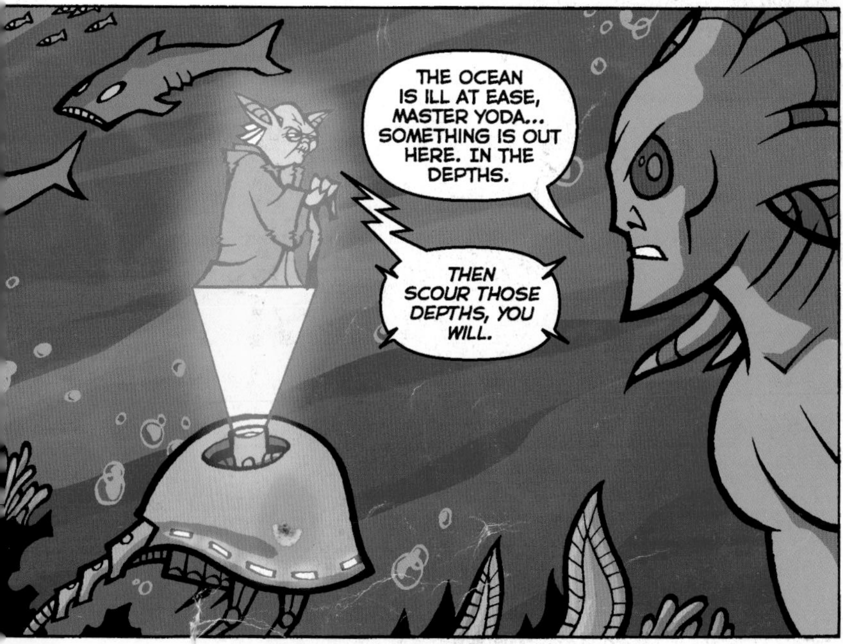
THE OCEAN IS ILL AT EASE, MASTER YODA... SOMETHING IS OUT HERE. IN THE DEPTHS.
THEN SCOUR THOSE DEPTHS, YOU WILL.

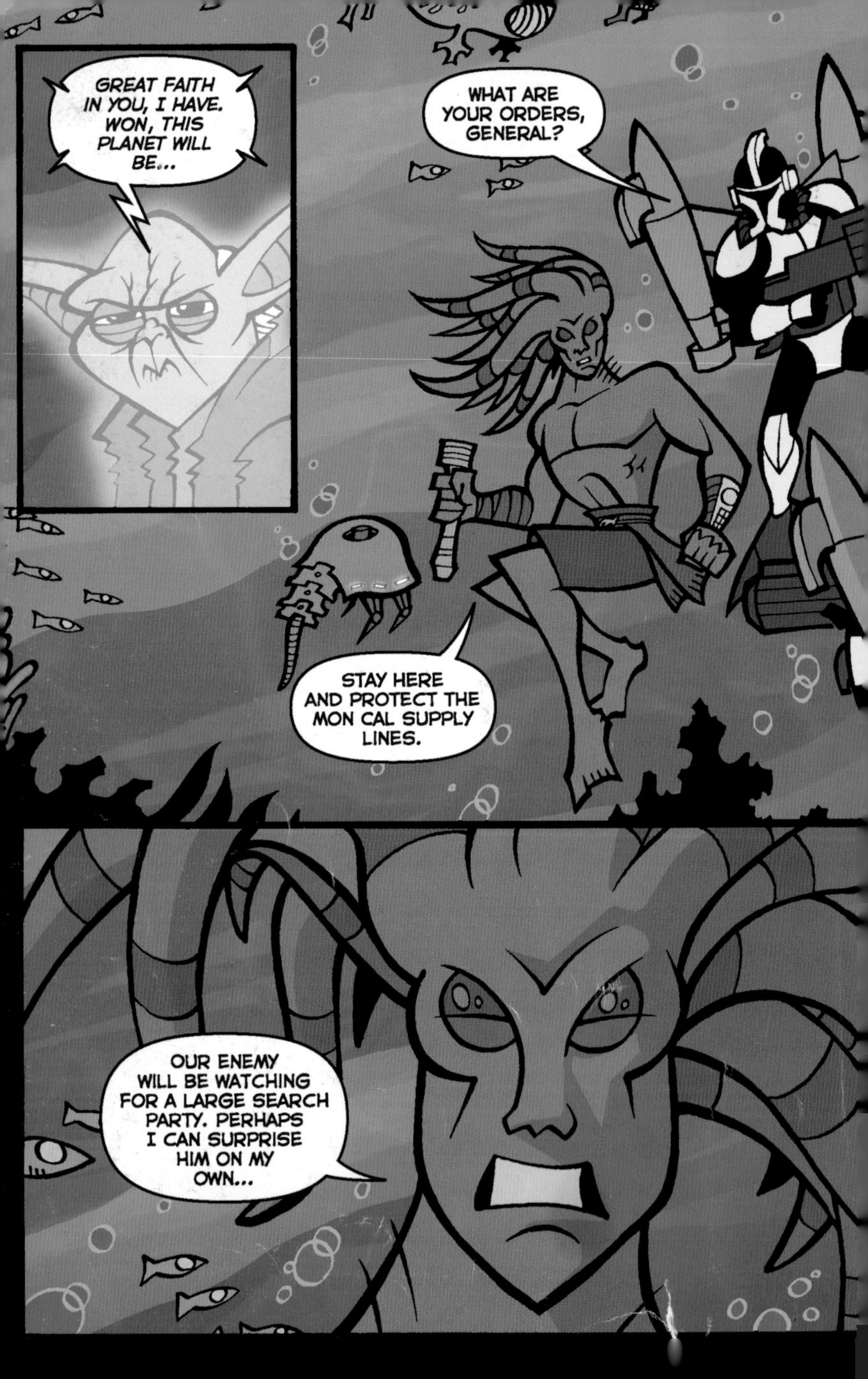
GREAT FAITH IN YOU, I HAVE. WON, THIS PLANET WILL BE...
WHAT ARE YOUR ORDERS, GENERAL?
STAY HERE AND PROTECT THE MON CAL SUPPLY LINES.
OUR ENEMY WILL BE WATCHING FOR A LARGE SEARCH PARTY. PERHAPS I CAN SURPRISE HIM ON MY OWN...

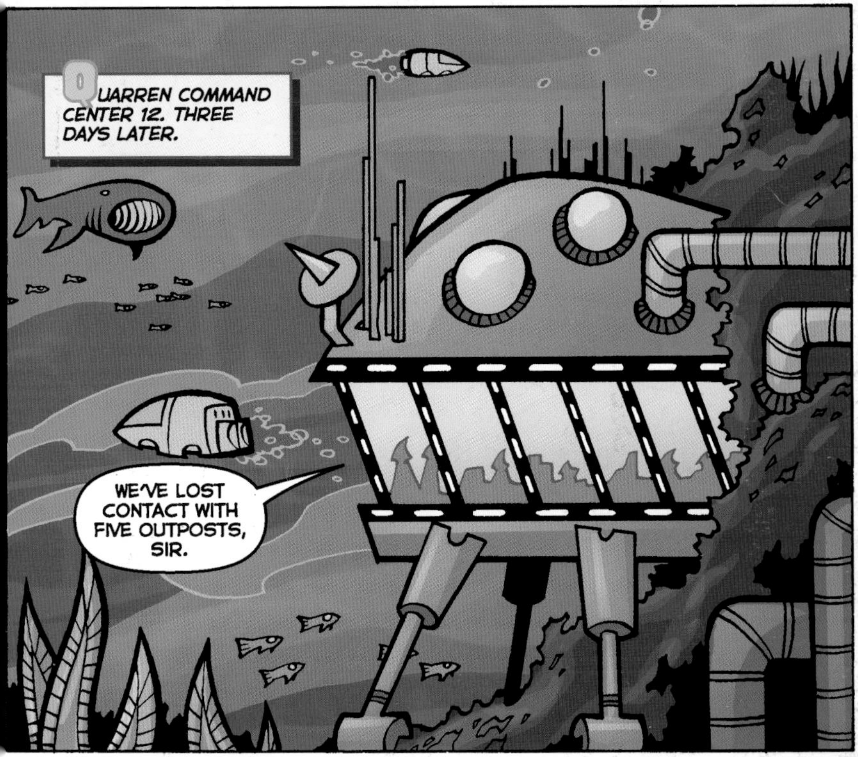
QUARREN COMMAND CENTER 12. THREE DAYS LATER.
WE'VE LOST CONTACT WITH FIVE OUTPOSTS, SIR.

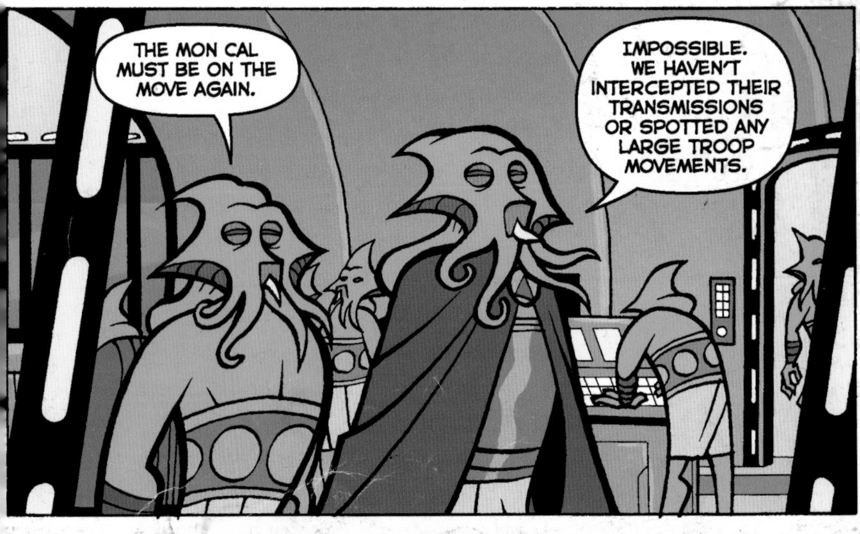
THE MON CAL MUST BE ON THE MOVE AGAIN.
IMPOSSIBLE. WE HAVEN'T INTERCEPTED THEIR TRANSMISSIONS OR SPOTTED ANY LARGE TROOP MOVEMENTS.

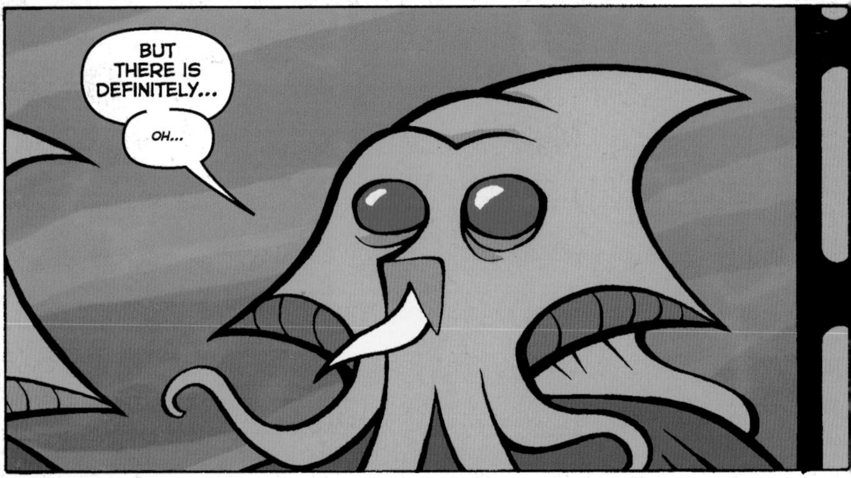
BUT THERE IS DEFINITELY...
OH...

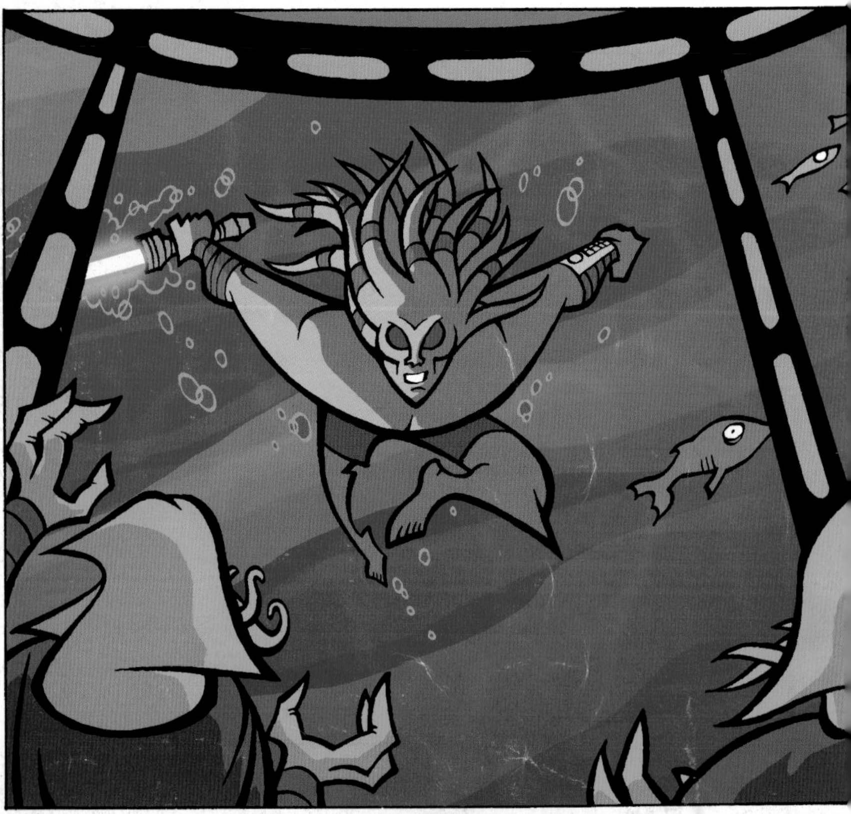

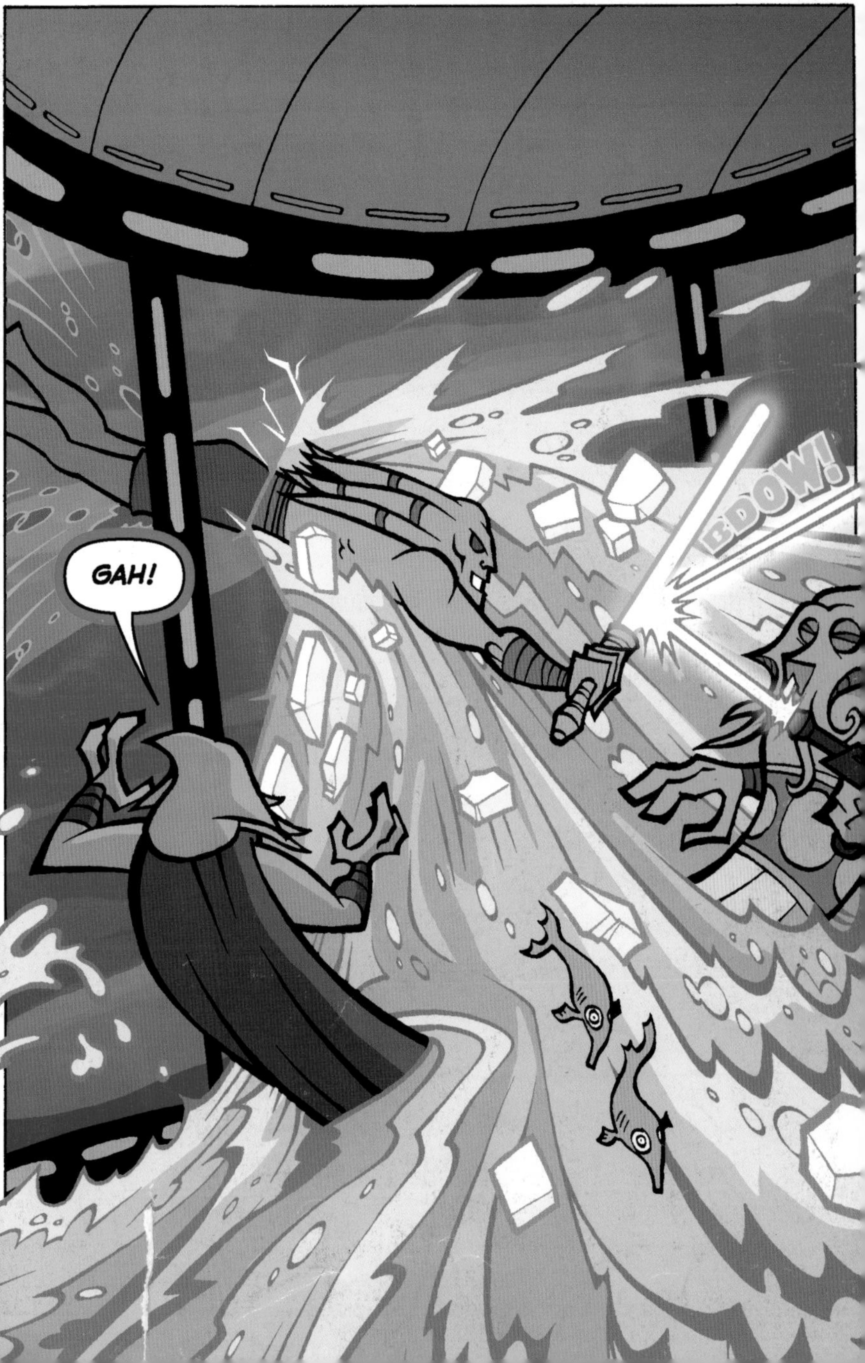
GAH!
BDOW!

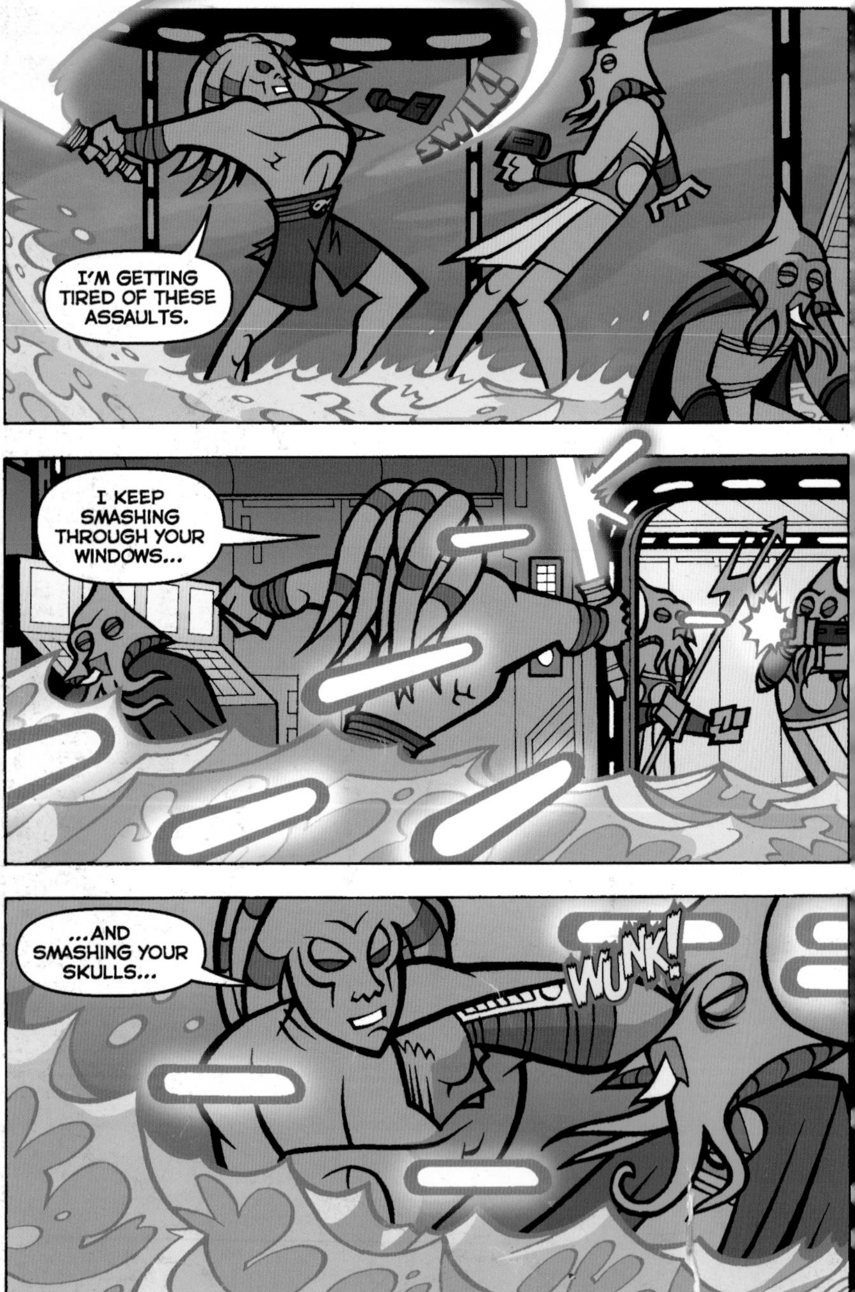
SWIK!
I'M GETTING TIRED OF THESE ASSAULTS.
I KEEP SMASHING THROUGH YOUR WINDOWS...
...AND SMASHING YOUR SKULLS...
WUNK!

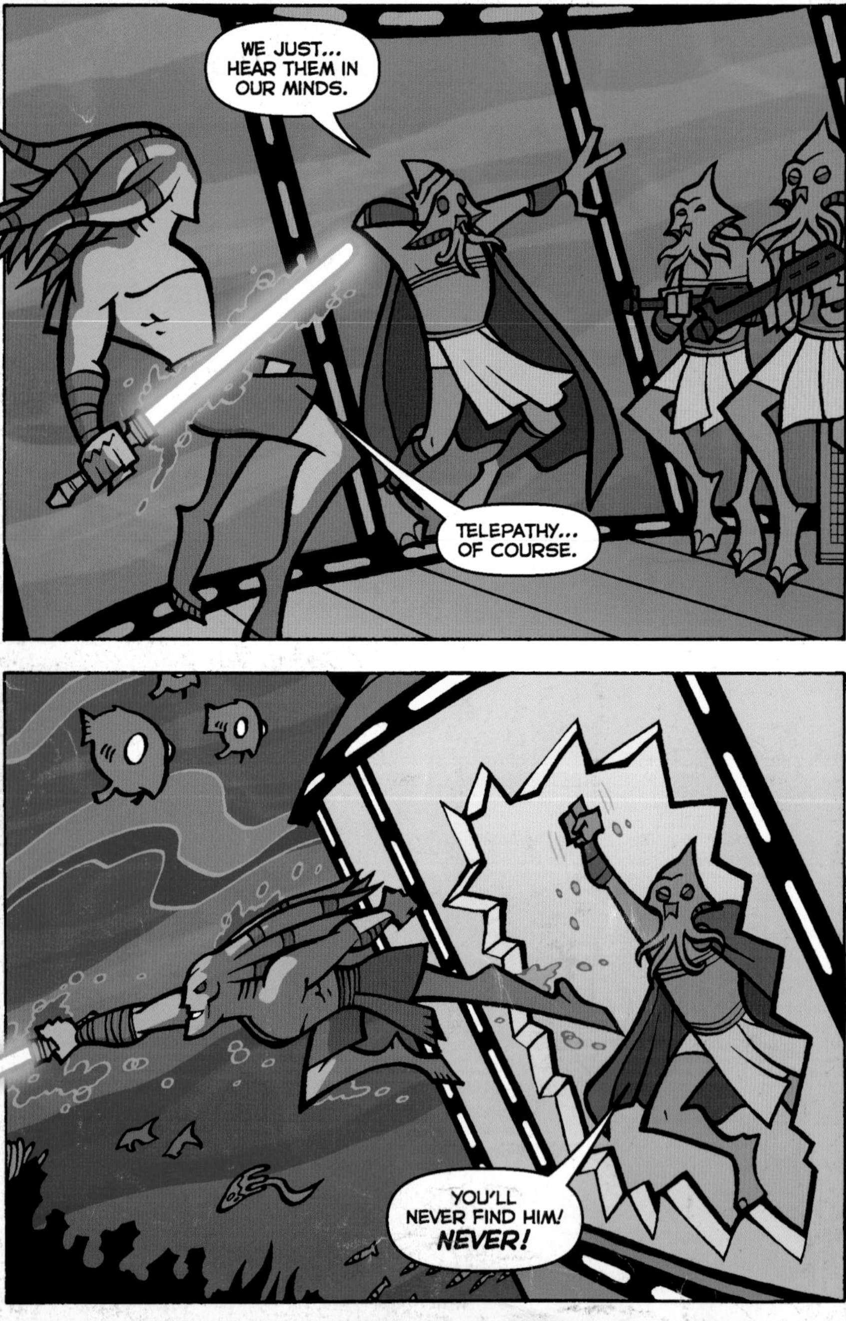
WE JUST... HEAR THEM IN OUR MINDS.
TELEPATHY... OF COURSE.
YOU'LL NEVER FIND HIM! NEVER!

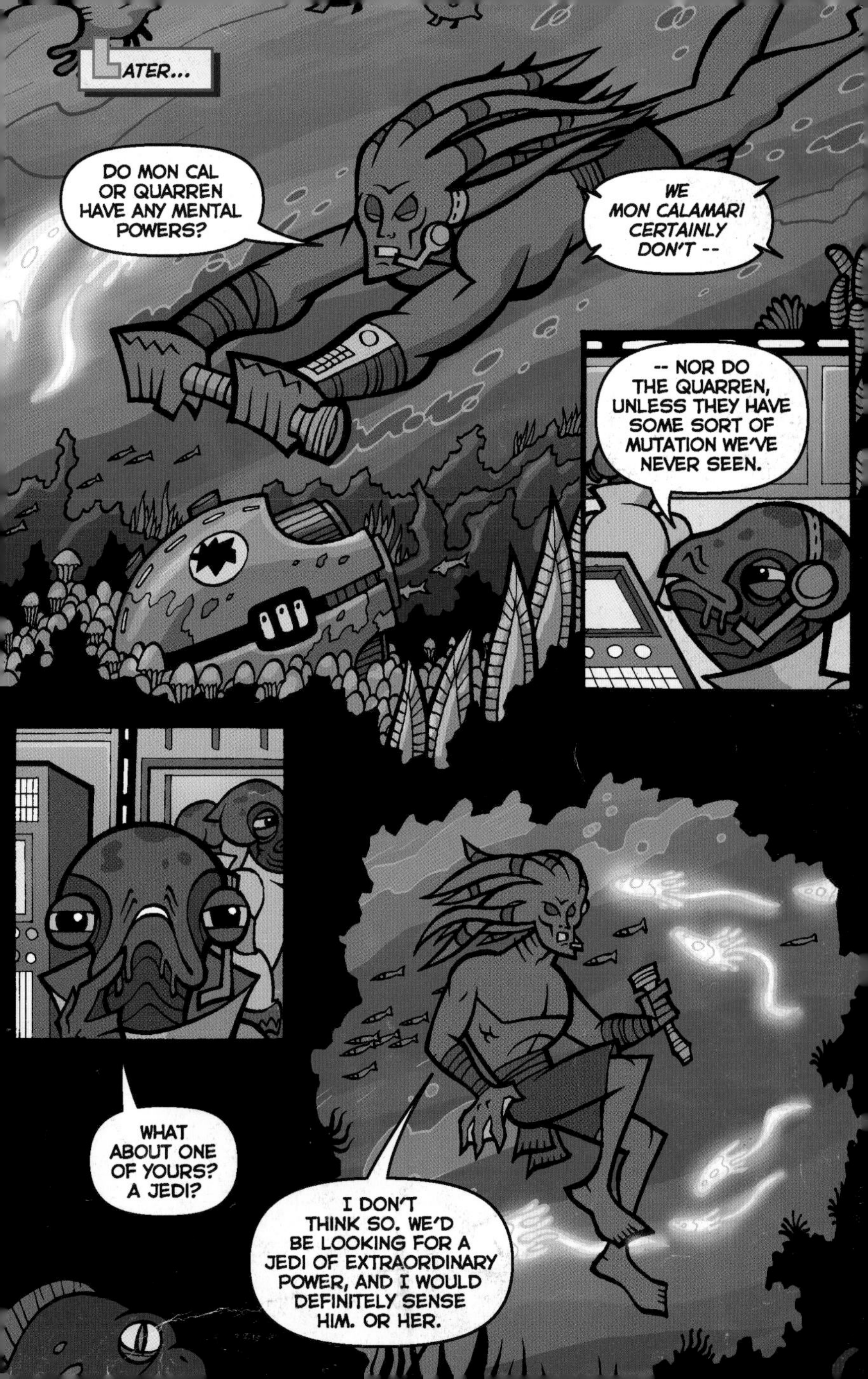
LATER...
DO MON CAL OR QUARREN HAVE ANY MENTAL POWERS?
WE MON CALAMARI CERTAINLY DON'T --
-- NOR DO THE QUARREN, UNLESS THEY HAVE SOME SORT OF MUTATION WE'VE NEVER SEEN.
WHAT ABOUT ONE OF YOURS? A JEDI?
I DON'T THINK SO. WE'D BE LOOKING FOR A JEDI OF EXTRAORDINARY POWER, AND I WOULD DEFINITELY SENSE HIM. OR HER.

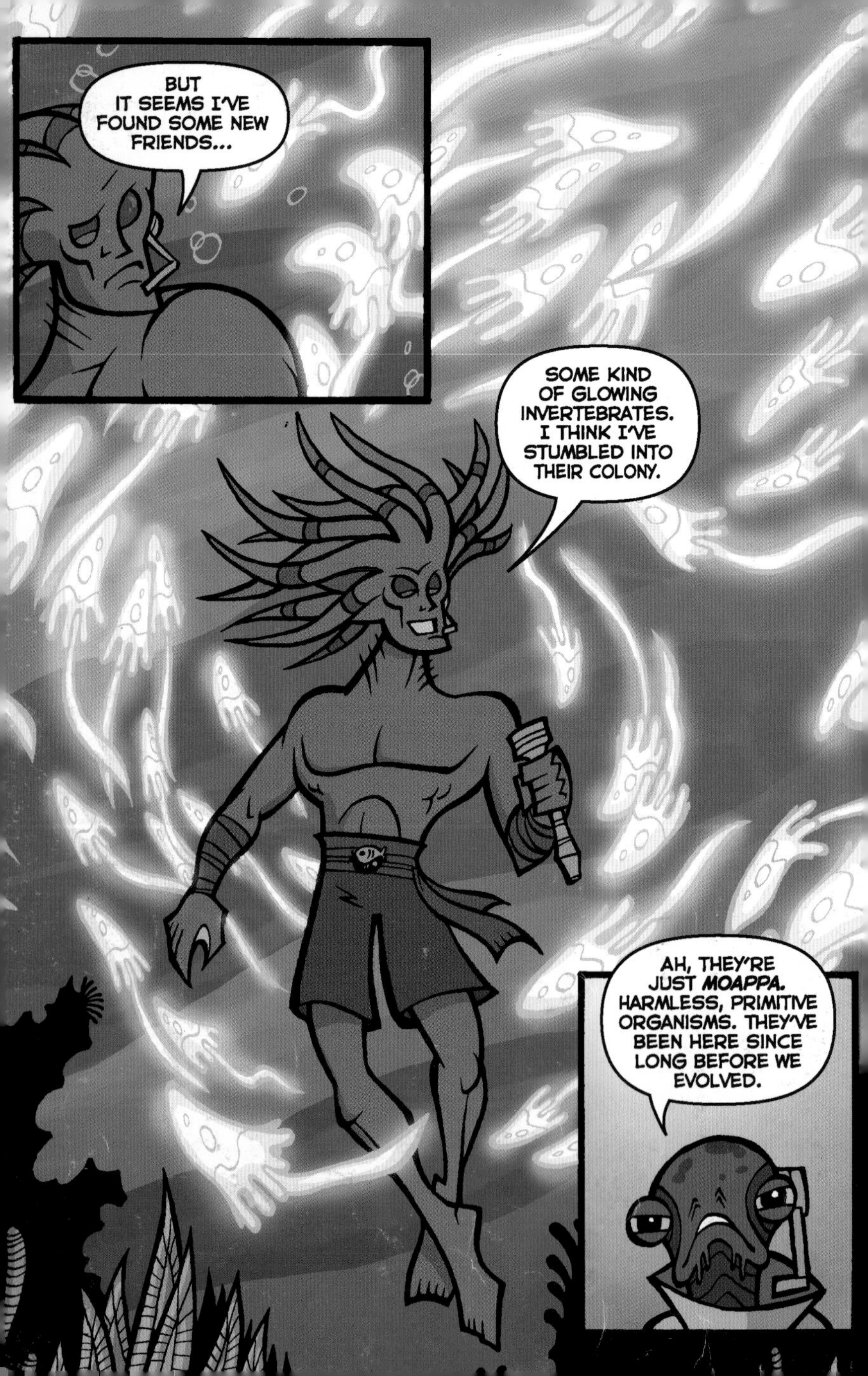
BUT IT SEEMS I'VE FOUND SOME NEW FRIENDS...
SOME KIND OF GLOWING INVERTEBRATES. I THINK I'VE STUMBLED INTO THEIR COLONY.
AH, THEY'RE JUST *MOAPPA.* HARMLESS, PRIMITIVE ORGANISMS. THEY'VE BEEN HERE SINCE LONG BEFORE WE EVOLVED.

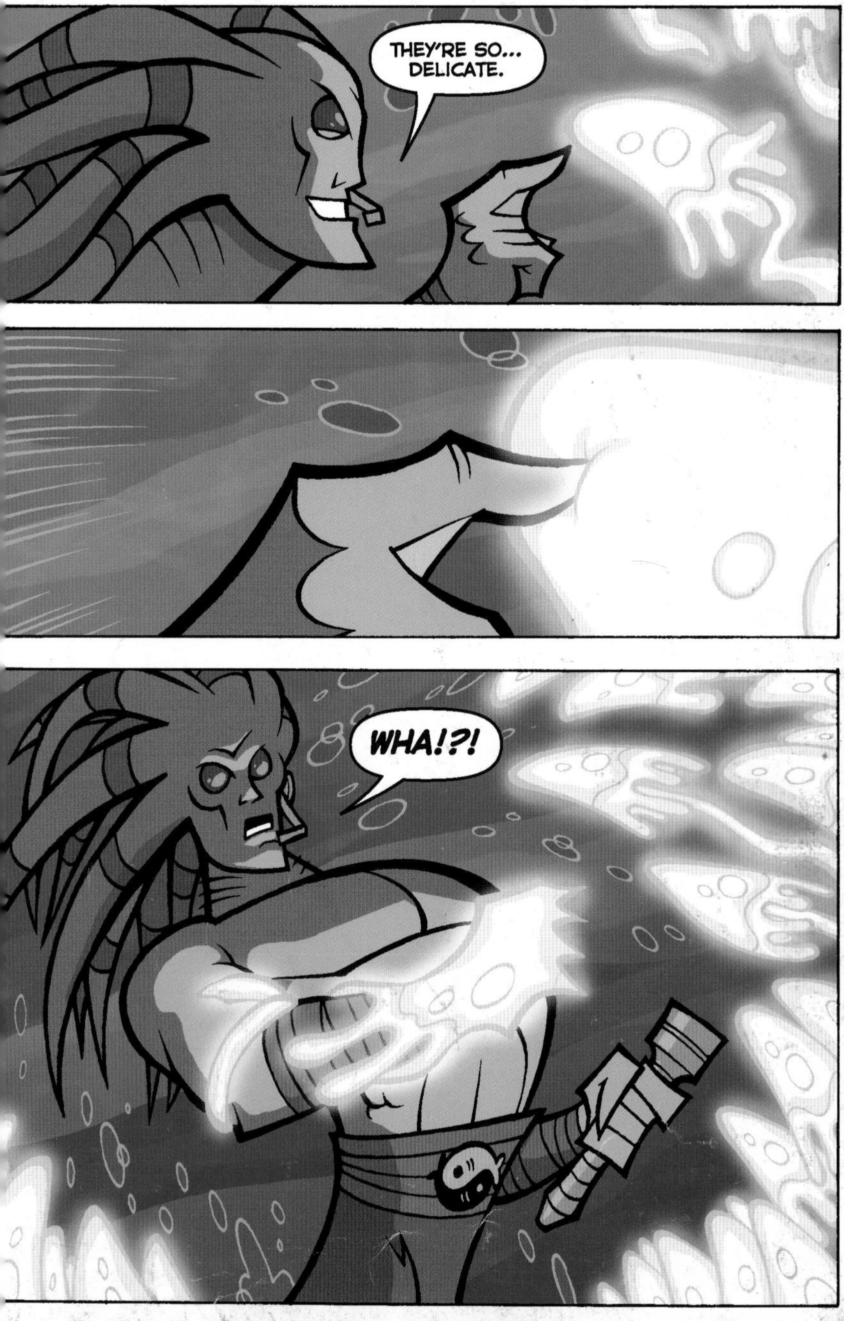
THEY'RE SO... DELICATE.
WHA!?!

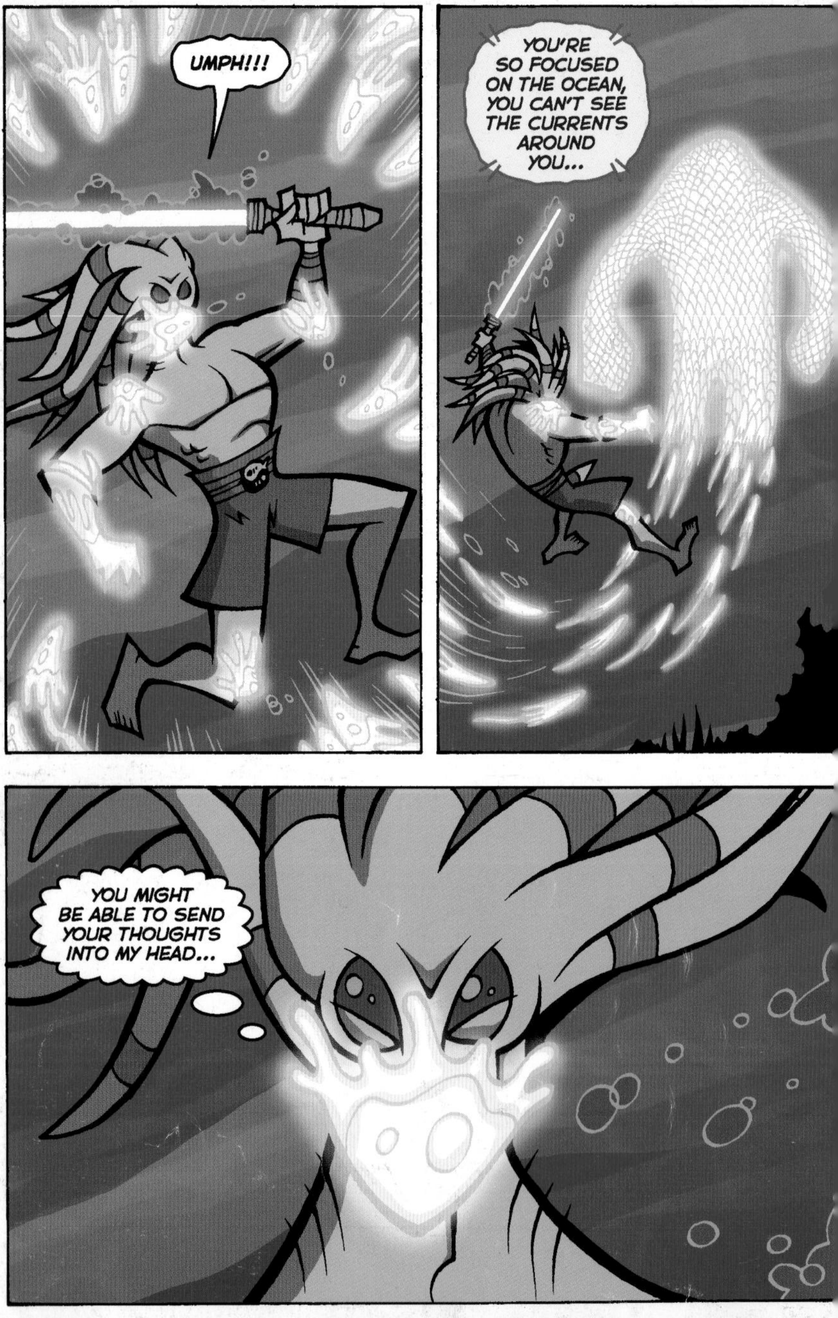
UMPH!!!
YOU'RE SO FOCUSED ON THE OCEAN, YOU CAN'T SEE THE CURRENTS AROUND YOU...
YOU MIGHT BE ABLE TO SEND YOUR THOUGHTS INTO MY HEAD...

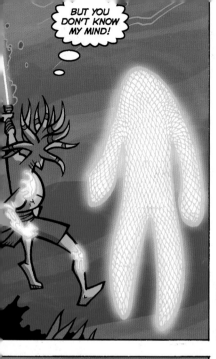

BUT YOU DON'T KNOW MY MIND!

WE CAN REACT MORE QUICKLY THAN YOU CAN THINK.

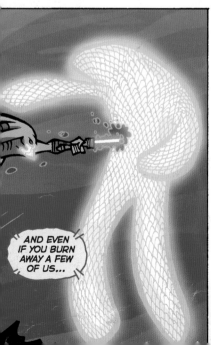

AND EVEN IF YOU BURN AWAY A FEW OF US...

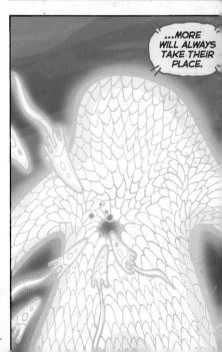

...MORE WILL ALWAYS TAKE THEIR PLACE.

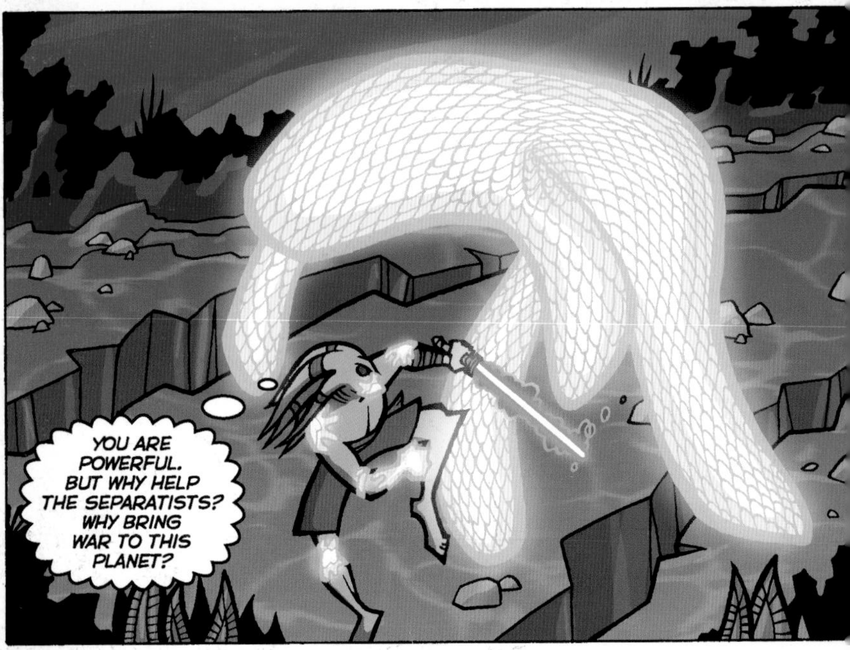
YOU ARE POWERFUL. BUT WHY HELP THE SEPARATISTS? WHY BRING WAR TO THIS PLANET?

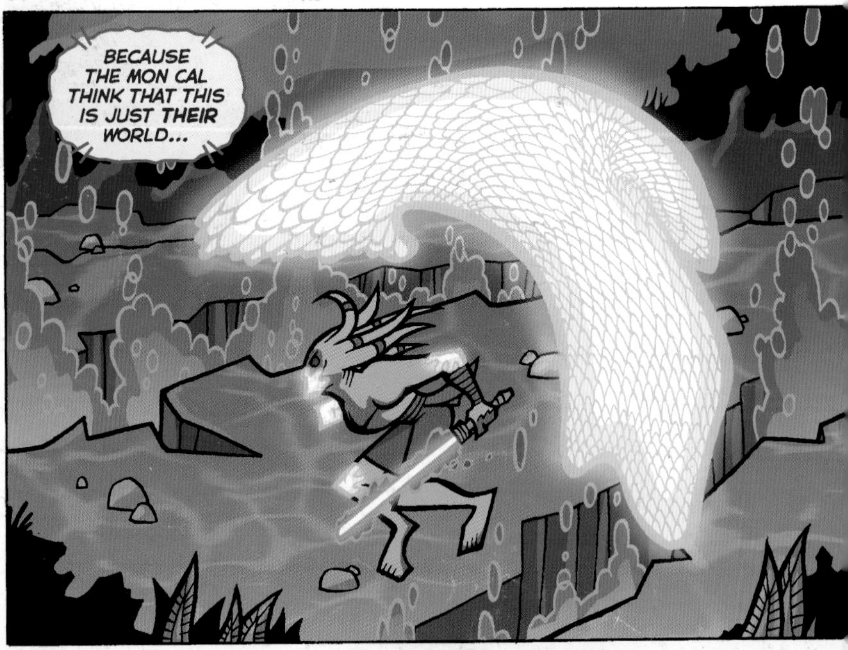
BECAUSE THE MON CAL THINK THAT THIS IS JUST THEIR WORLD...

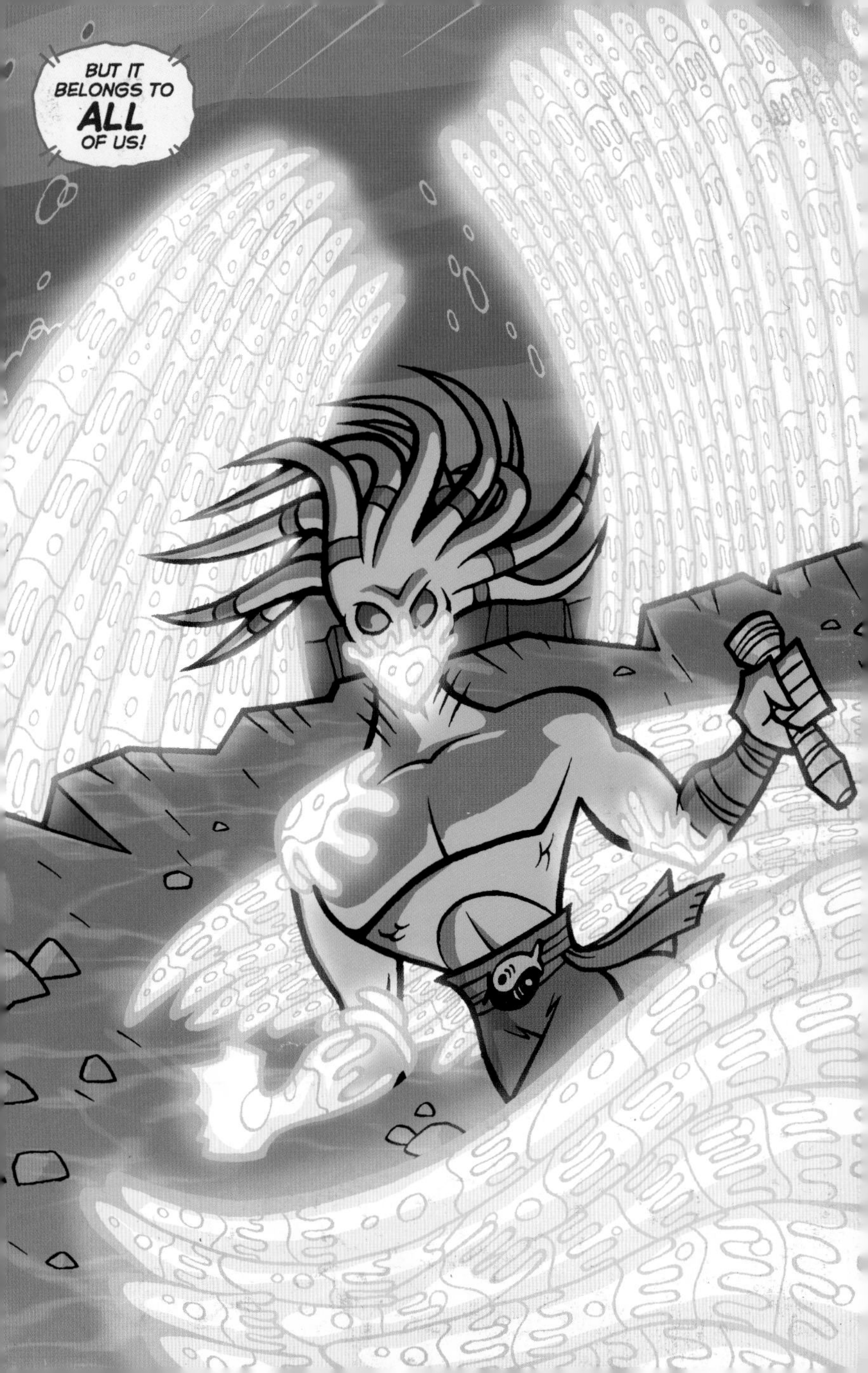
BUT IT BELONGS TO ALL OF US!

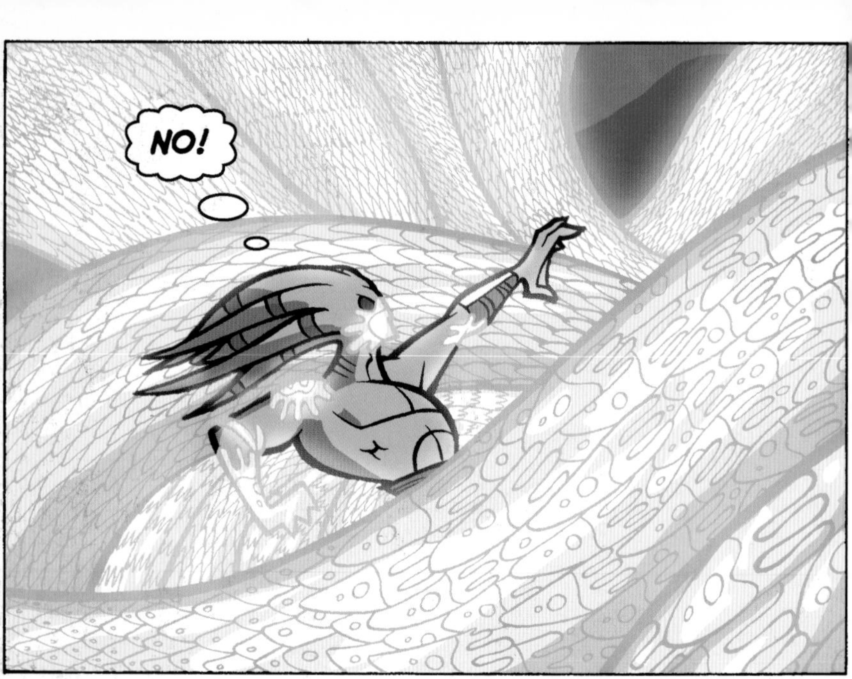
NO!

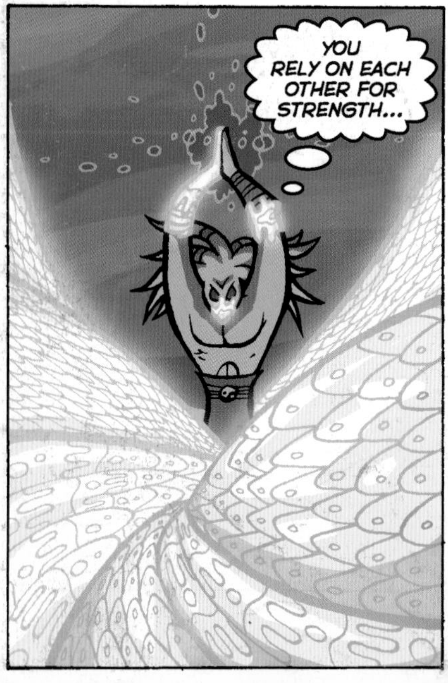
YOU RELY ON EACH OTHER FOR STRENGTH...

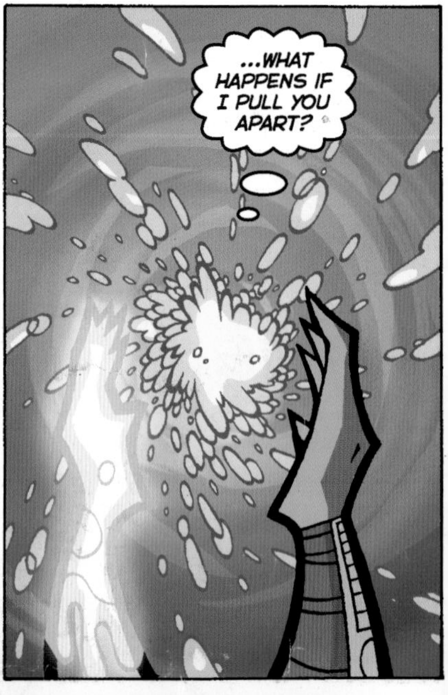
...WHAT HAPPENS IF I PULL YOU APART?

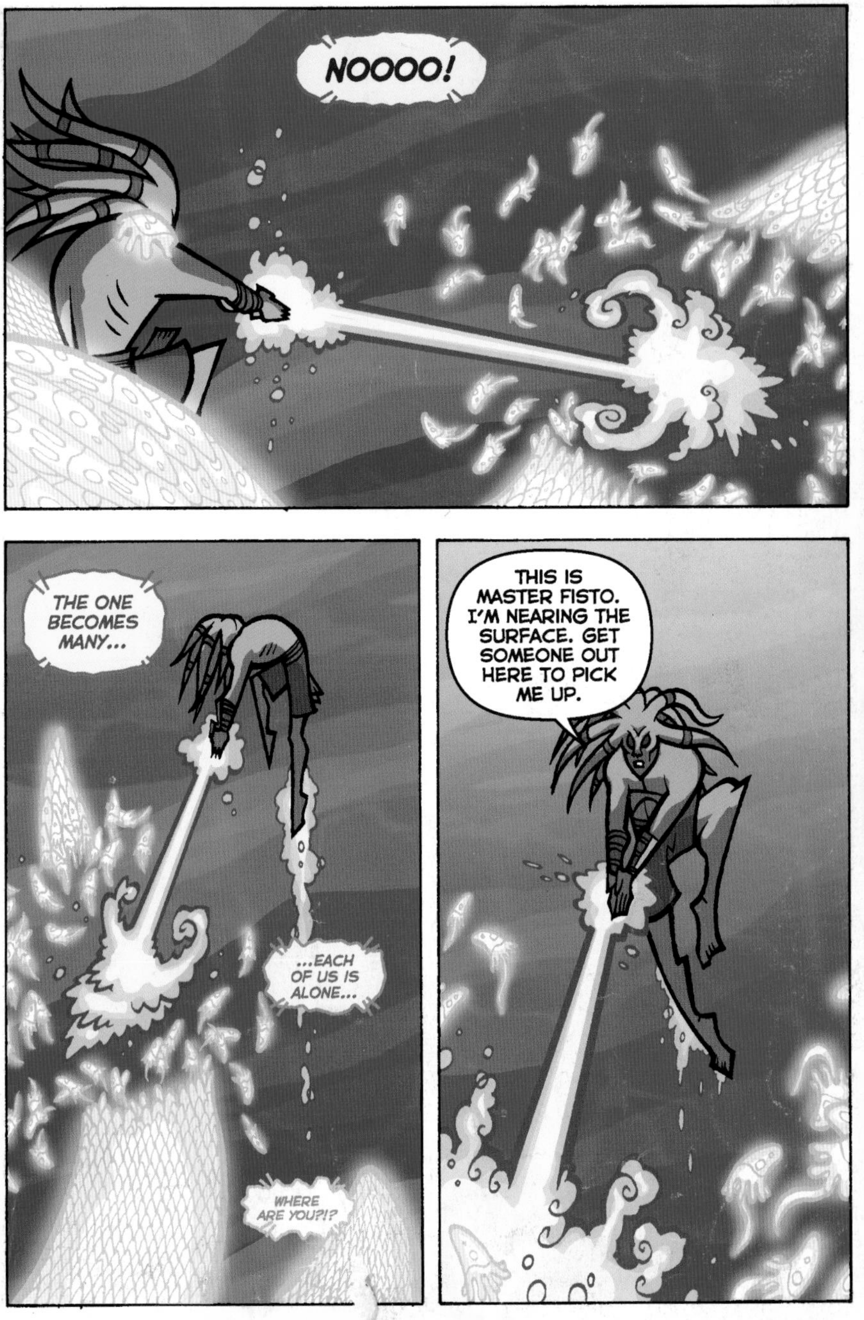
NOOOO!
THE ONE BECOMES MANY...
...EACH OF US IS ALONE...
WHERE ARE YOU?!?
THIS IS MASTER FISTO. I'M NEARING THE SURFACE. GET SOMEONE OUT HERE TO PICK ME UP.

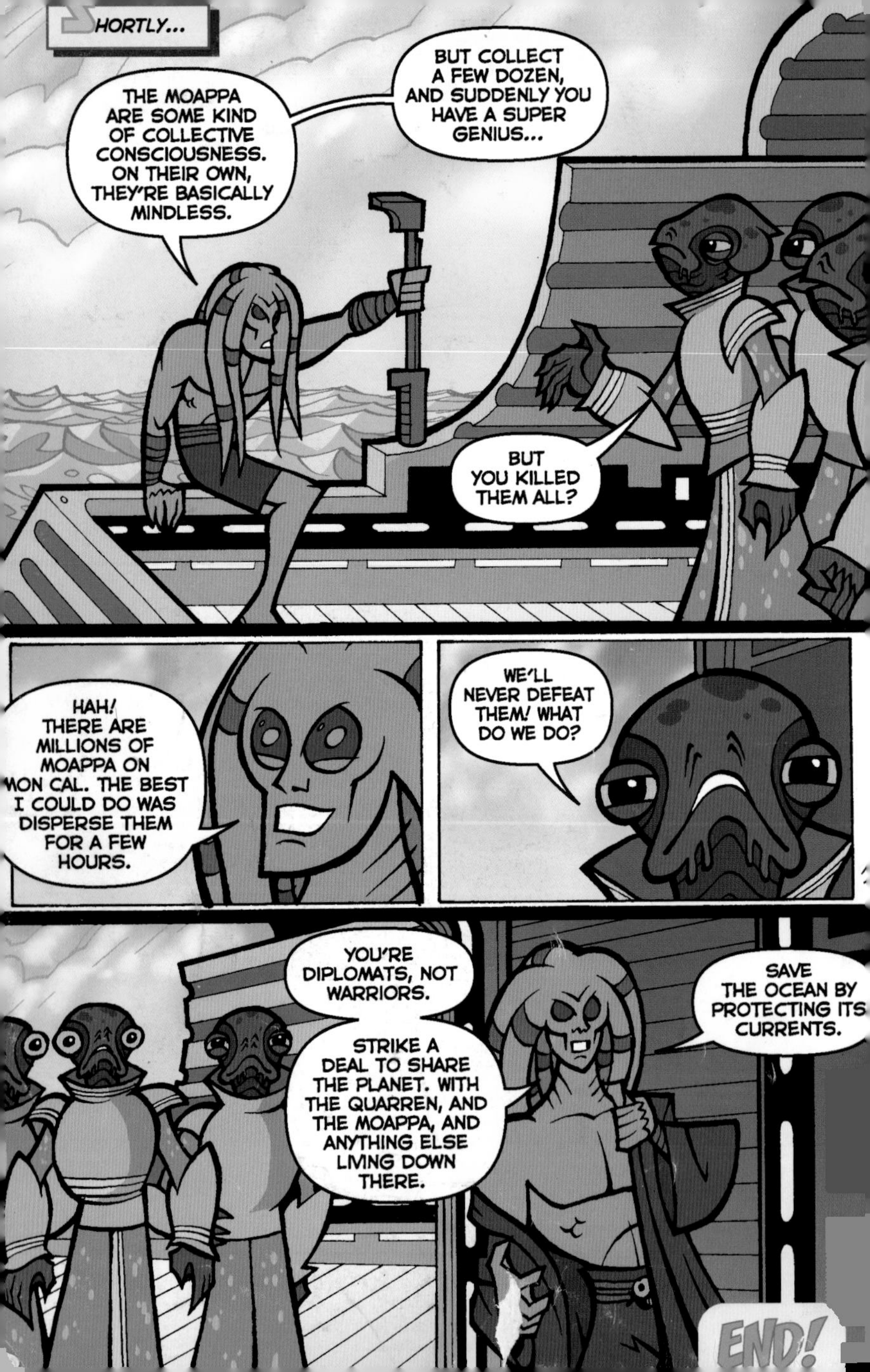
SHORTLY...
THE MOAPPA ARE SOME KIND OF COLLECTIVE CONSCIOUSNESS. ON THEIR OWN, THEY'RE BASICALLY MINDLESS.
BUT COLLECT A FEW DOZEN, AND SUDDENLY YOU HAVE A SUPER GENIUS...
BUT YOU KILLED THEM ALL?
HAH! THERE ARE MILLIONS OF MOAPPA ON MON CAL. THE BEST I COULD DO WAS DISPERSE THEM FOR A FEW HOURS.
WE'LL NEVER DEFEAT THEM! WHAT DO WE DO?
YOU'RE DIPLOMATS, NOT WARRIORS.
STRIKE A DEAL TO SHARE THE PLANET. WITH THE QUARREN, AND THE MOAPPA, AND ANYTHING ELSE LIVING DOWN THERE.
SAVE THE OCEAN BY PROTECTING ITS CURRENTS.
END!

STAR WARS®
CLONE WARS ADVENTURES

Don't miss any of the action-packed adventures of your favorite STAR WARS® characters, availble at comics shops and bookstores in a galaxy near you!

STAR WARS
CLONE WARS
ADVENTURES
Vol 1
THREE NEW STORIES! ALL-JEDI ACTION!

Volume 1
ISBN: 1-59307-243-0 / $6.95

STAR WARS
CLONE WARS
ADVENTURES
THREE TALES OF HYPERKINETIC JEDI ACTION!
Vol 2

Volume 2
ISBN: 1-59307-271-6 / $6.95

STAR WARS
CLONE WARS
ADVENTURES
FOUR TALES OF SINISTER SEPARATIST SCHEMING AND ROCKING REPUBLIC COMBAT!
Vol 3

Volume 3
ISBN: 1-59307-307-0 / $6.95

STAR WARS
CLONE WARS
ADVENTURES
FOUR RIVETING ADVENTURES IN ONE FANTASTIC VOLUME!
Vol 4

Volume 4
ISBN: 1-59307-402-6 / $6.95

To find a comics shop in your area, call 1-888-266-4226

For more information or to order direct: • On the web: darkhorse.com • E-mail: mailorder@darkhorse.com

• Phone: 1-800-862-0052 or (503) 652-9701 Mon.-Sat. 9 A.M. to 5 P.M. Pacific Time

***Prices and availability subject to change without notice**

STAR WARS®
CLONE WARS

Experience all the excitement and drama of the Clone Wars! Look for these trade paperbacks at a comics shop or book store near you!

STAR WARS
CLONE WARS
VOLUME 1
The Defense of Kamino
and other tales

Volume 1
ISBN: 1-56971-962-4 / $14.95

STAR WARS
CLONE WARS
VOLUME 2
Victories and Sacrifices

Volume 2
ISBN: 1-56971-969-1 / $14.95

STAR WARS
CLONE WARS
VOLUME 3
Last Stand on Jabiim

Volume 3
ISBN: 1-59307-006-3 / $14.95

STAR WARS
CLONE WARS
VOLUME 4
Light and Dark

Volume 4
ISBN: 1-59307-195-7 / $16.95

ALSO AVAILABLE

Volume 5
ISBN: 1-59307-273-2 / $14.95

Volume 6
ISBN: 1-59307-352-6 / $17.95

To find a comics shop in your area, call 1-888-266-4226
For more information or to order direct: • On the web: darkhorse.com • E-mail: mailorder@darkhorse.com
• Phone: 1-800-862-0052 or (503) 652-9701 Mon.-Sat. 9 A.M. to 5 P.M. Pacific Time
***Prices and availability subject to change without notice**

STAR WARS®

TIMELINE OF TRADE PAPERBACKS AND GRAPHIC NOVELS!

OLD REPUBLIC ERA:
25,000-1000 YEARS BEFORE
STAR WARS: A NEW HOPE

Tales of the Jedi—
Knights of the Old Republic
ISBN: 1-56971-020-1 $14.95

Dark Lords of the Sith
ISBN: 1-56971-095-3 $17.95

The Sith War
ISBN: 1-56971-173-9 $17.95

The Golden Age of the Sith
ISBN: 1-56971-229-8 $16.95

The Freedon Nadd Uprising
ISBN: 1-56971-307-3 $5.95

The Fall of the Sith Empire
ISBN: 1-56971-320-0 $15.95

Redemption
ISBN: 1-56971-535-1 $14.95

Jedi vs. Sith
ISBN: 1-56971-649-8 $17.95

RISE OF THE EMPIRE ERA:
1000-0 YEARS BEFORE
STAR WARS: A NEW HOPE

The Stark Hyperspace War
ISBN: 1-56971-985-3 $12.95

Prelude to Rebellion
ISBN: 1-56971-448-7 $14.95

Jedi Council—Acts of War
ISBN: 1-56971-539-4 $12.95

Darth Maul
ISBN: 1-56971-542-4 $12.95

Jedi Council—
Emissaries to Malastare
ISBN: 1-56971-545-9 $15.95

Episode I—
The Phantom Menace
ISBN: 1-56971-359-6 $12.95

Episode I—
The Phantom Menace Adventures
ISBN: 1-56971-443-6 $12.95

Outlander
ISBN: 1-56971-514-9 $14.95

Star Wars: Jango Fett—
Open Seasons
ISBN: 1-56971-671-4 $12.95

The Bounty Hunters
ISBN: 1-56971-467-3 $12.95

Twilight
ISBN: 1-56971-558-0 $12.95

The Hunt for Aurra Sing
ISBN: 1-56971-651-X $12.95

Darkness
ISBN: 1-56971-659-5 $12.95

The Rite of Passage
ISBN: 1-59307-042-X $12.95

Episode II—Attack of the Clones
ISBN: 1-56971-609-9 $17.95

Clone Wars Volume 1:
The Defense of Kamino
ISBN: 1-56971-962-4 $14.95

Clone Wars Volume 2:
Victories and Sacrifices
ISBN: 1-56971-969-1 $14.95

Clone Wars Adventures Volume 1
ISBN: 1-59307-243-0 $6.95

Clone Wars Volume 3:
Last Stand on Jabiim
ISBN: 1-59307-006-3 $14.95

Clone Wars Volume 4: Light and Dark
ISBN: 1-59307-195-7 $16.95

Droids—The Kalarba Adventures
ISBN: 1-56971-064-3 $17.95

Droids—Rebellion
ISBN: 1-56971-224-7 $14.95

Classic Star Wars—
Han Solo At Stars' End
ISBN: 1-56971-254-9 $6.95

Boba Fett—Enemy of The Empire
ISBN: 1-56971-407-X $12.95

Dark Forces—
Soldier for the Empire GSA
ISBN: 1-56971-348-0 $14.95

Mara Jade—By the Emperor's Hand
ISBN: 1-56971-401-0 $15.95

Underworld
ISBN: 1-56971-618-8 $15.95

Empire Volume 1: Betrayal
ISBN: 1-56971-964-0 $12.95

Empire Volume 2: Darklighter
ISBN: 1-56971-975-6 $17.95

REBELLION ERA:
0-5 YEARS AFTER
STAR WARS: A NEW HOPE

Classic Star Wars, Volume 1:
In Deadly Pursuit
ISBN: 1-56971-109-7 $16.95

Classic Star Wars, Volume 2:
The Rebel Storm
ISBN: 1-56971-106-2 $16.95

Classic Star Wars, Volume 3:
Escape to Hoth
ISBN: 1-56971-093-7 $16.95

Classic Star Wars—
The Early Adventures
ISBN: 1-56971-178-X $19.95

Jabba the Hutt—The Art of the Deal
ISBN: 1-56971-310-3 $9.95

Vader's Quest
ISBN: 1-56971-415-0 $11.95

Splinter of the Mind's Eye
ISBN: 1-56971-223-9 $14.95

A Long Time Ago... Volume 1:
Doomworld
ISBN: 1-56971-754-0 $29.95

A Long Time Ago... Volume 2:
Dark Encounters
ISBN: 1-56971-785-0 $29.95

A Long Time Ago... Volume 3:
Resurrection of Evil
ISBN: 1-56971-786-9 $29.95

A Long Time Ago... Volume 4:
Screams in the Void
ISBN: 1-56971-787-7 $29.95

A Long Time Ago... Volume 5:
Fool's Bounty
ISBN: 1-56971-906-3 $29.95

A Long Time Ago... Volume 6:
Wookiee World
ISBN: 1-56971-907-1 $29.95

A Long Time Ago... Volume 7:
Far, Far Away
ISBN: 1-56971-908-X $29.95

Battle of the Bounty Hunters
Pop-Up Book
ISBN: 1-56971-129-1 $17.95

Shadows of the Empire
ISBN: 1-56971-183-6 $17.95

The Empire Strikes Back—
The Special Edition
ISBN: 1-56971-234-4 $9.95

Return of the Jedi—The Special Edition
ISBN: 1-56971-235-2 $9.95

NEW REPUBLIC ERA:
5-25 YEARS AFTER
STAR WARS: A NEW HOPE

X-Wing Rouge Squadron
The Phantom Affair
ISBN: 1-56971-251-4 $12.95

Battleground Tatooine
ISBN: 1-56971-276-X $12.95

The Warrior Princess
ISBN: 1-56971-330-8 $12.95

Requiem for a Rogue
ISBN: 1-56971-331-6 $12.95

In the Empire's Service
ISBN: 1-56971-383-9 $12.95

Blood and Honor
ISBN: 1-56971-387-1 $12.95

Masquerade
ISBN: 1-56971-487-8 $12.95

Mandatory Retirement
ISBN: 1-56971-492-4 $12.95

Shadows of the Empire
Evolution
ISBN: 1-56971-441-X $14.95

Heir to the Empire
ISBN: 1-56971-202-6 $19.95

Dark Force Rising
ISBN: 1-56971-269-7 $17.95

The Last Command
ISBN: 1-56971-378-2 $17.95

Dark Empire
ISBN: 1-59307-039-X $16.95

Dark Empire II
ISBN: 1-56971-119-4 $17.95

Empire's End
ISBN: 1-56971-306-5 $5.95

Boba Fett—Death, Lies, & Treachery
ISBN: 1-56971-311-1 $12.95

Crimson Empire
ISBN: 1-56971-355-3 $17.95

Crimson Empire II—Council of Blood
ISBN: 1-56971-410-X $17.95

Jedi Academy—Leviathan
ISBN: 1-56971-456-8 $11.95

Union
ISBN: 1-56971-464-9 $12.95

NEW JEDI ORDER ERA:
25+ YEARS AFTER
STAR WARS: A NEW HOPE

Chewbacca
ISBN: 1-56971-515-7 $12.95

INFINITIES:
DOES NOT APPLY TO TIMELINE

Infinities — A New Hope
ISBN: 1-56971-648-X $12.95

Infinities—The Empire Strikes Back
ISBN: 1-56971-904-7 $12.95

Infinities—Return of the Jedi
ISBN: 1-59307-206-6 $12.95

Star Wars Tales Volume 1
ISBN: 1-56971-619-6 $19.95

Star Wars Tales Volume 2
ISBN: 1-56971-757-5 $19.95

Star Wars Tales Volume 3
ISBN: 1-56971-836-9 $19.95

Star Wars Tales Volume 4
ISBN: 1-56971-989-6 $19.95